1025

Trondheim
Nidaros

Finland

Sweden

Russia

Oslo
Sarpsborg
Upsala
Stavanger
Tunsberg

Denmark

The King's Men

Alan Boucher

The King's Men

A STORY OF ST. OLAF OF NORWAY

ILLUSTRATED BY
Emil Weiss

A CLARION BOOK

DOUBLEDAY & COMPANY, INC.,   GARDEN CITY, NEW YORK

BURNS & OATES LTD., LONDON

Library of Congress Catalog Card Number 62–16743
Copyright © 1962 by Alan Boucher
All Rights Reserved
Printed in the United States of America
First Edition

For my son
Robin Gunnar Olafur

King Olaf Tryggvason then went to Upland and there proclaimed the true faith. It was in the third year of his reign. The king was received there with feasting, and at the feast all the people were baptized. At that time Olaf Haraldsson was baptized, with the others. He was then three years old, and King Olaf Tryggvason himself was his godfather, while Bishop Sigurd baptized him. And as the boy was taken up from the font, Hrani spoke thus, three times: "Light, light, light."

(from the *Saga of King Olaf Haraldsson*)

CONTENTS

The Viking's Dream

The mountains that guarded the entrance to the Trond-heimsfjord were shrouded in a mist of rain as the *Heron* beat upwind toward Agdaness. Once level with the point, Thorarin the Shipmaster ordered the boatswain to lower the great square sail, and oars were run out through the ports. Helgi, standing up in the stern beside his uncle,

watched the high, curved bow swing round as the shipmaster leaned on the steering oar. To the boy it seemed
as if their new course would take them dangerously close
to the white breakers offshore, but his uncle must have
read the thought, for he reached across with his free
hand to pat his shoulder.

"Never fear, Helgi," he said. "Did I not promise your
mother that I would see you safely to Norway? The
voyage is all but over, and within these four hours or so
we shall be in a safe anchorage."

Helgi returned his uncle's smile and drew his woolen
cloak more closely about him. It had been a long and
wearisome journey since they had left Islefirth in the
north of Iceland, that summer of the year 1025, with
contrary winds for much of the way—a mere trifle, maybe,
to seasoned shipmen such as Uncle Thorarin and his
crew, but a trial to Helgi, who, at the age of eleven,
had never before ventured beyond the sheltered waters
of his own fjord in his father's rowing boat. And yet he
knew that, in spite of the cold and wetness and the sea-
sickness, he had done well and his uncle was not dis-
pleased with him. After all, even this King Olaf, about
whom Thorarin never tired of speaking, had been a full
twelve winters old when he set out on his first viking
raid. Helgi thought, *I was not born with a king's name,
but I am the son of a free man and an Icelander, and I
can look any Norwegian in the face.* For, truth to tell,
it was not the breakers on the rocks of Agdaness alone
that were making him frown, but also the thought of
what the future might hold in store for him beyond that
safe anchorage promised by his uncle.

He looked up at the gulls that wheeled, screaming,

about their masthead, and said, "Uncle, maybe the king will not want to have me in his service."

Thorarin was silent for a moment, intent on steering as the cross seas lifted and swept them toward the danger mark on the south side of the channel, and he called to the boatswain to shorten the oar stroke. Then he glanced at Helgi from under his bushy eyebrows that were rimed with spray and said, "King Olaf will do that much for me, and more, if I should ask it of him. Have I not told you that I sailed with him once as far as Spain, and might have sailed farther but for his dream that brought him home to Norway?"

"I remember something about it," said Helgi. "But that was long ago, wasn't it?"

"All of ten years," replied Thorarin shortly. "I have done him a good service more than once since that time, though."

At once Helgi's thoughts were carried back to a distant childhood memory of a bright spring morning in Iceland many years ago, with the snow on the mountain-tops, and himself a little boy perched on the bow of his uncle's saddle. They were on their way to visit a small farm near the western shore of the Islefirth—he had been there since and knew now that it was called Calfskin; an odd name for a farm, he thought—and to this day he remembered the keen sense of disappointment with which he caught his first glimpse of the huddle of turf-roofed buildings with the mountain slope rising steeply behind it out of the green meadows and the glittering arc of the firth beyond.

"Why, Uncle, that's not a king's house," he had exclaimed indignantly, but his uncle had assured him that there was a king living there—the only king that had ever come to live in Iceland, he had said. But Helgi's disappointment at Calfskin had been nothing to his feelings on seeing the old man crouched sightless by the smoky hearth inside. Master Jon, the priest at Maddervale, had told him so many stories of kings in foreign lands, and especially of his hero, King Olaf Tryggvason of Norway, who had caused the Christian Faith to be brought to Iceland not so many years ago. Helgi *knew* what a king should look like, and this one had not even been wearing a crown. But as they rode away from Calfskin his uncle Thorarin had explained how a greater king, also named Olaf, had taken this old king's crown away from him, and his eyesight too, for kings sometimes had to do such things in their own defense.

The old blind king, Hrærek, had been one of a group of folk kings, each ruling over a small district in the southeast of Norway, his uncle had told him. Then Olaf Haraldsson had striven to make himself king over all Norway, but these folk kings had plotted against his life and government. Another would have had Hrærek put to death without a moment's thought, Thorarin had said; but not King Olaf. Because he was a great and good man, he had spared Hrærek's life and taken only his eyesight. And when the old man still went on plotting against him, the king had bidden Thorarin to bring him to Iceland, where he could do no hurt.

Helgi had thought with a shudder how wonderful and yet how cruel a thing it must be to be a king; and he had been glad that none had ever ruled in Iceland.

And now, within a few hours, he would be in the presence of that great king who, as his uncle Thorarin had told him, had risen over the heads of all earls and lesser kings to be undisputed master of Norway and liege lord of the isles of Orkney, Shetland and Faeroe across the sea, and who might have won Iceland, too, but for the suspicious pride of its chieftains. They, remembering how their ancestors had fled westward from Norway in the time of Harald Fairhair, because they would call no man lord, had rebuffed the king's friendly overtures. And yet his only desire had been God's glory and the good of the Christian Faith. Had he not given them wood for the new church at Thingvale, and sent many priests and clerks to teach them? Was it a wonder if Icelanders were not now enjoying the high favor that had always been given them by the king?

"But do not fear," Thorarin had said, "King Olaf is my good friend and he will receive us well."

Helgi hoped that his uncle was not mistaken, and stared with interest at the new land that was beginning to emerge from the mist on their starboard bow. It was a well-wooded land. The lower slopes of the hills were cloaked with dark fir trees and tall, slender silver birches —very different from the stunted scrub at home. Yet suddenly he felt homesick, longing with all his heart for his own familiar dale with its green meadows and the rushing stream and the gray-brown, rocky mountain slopes above the farmstead. This was a darker, older, more complicated land, with hidden dangers lurking in its deep, wooded valleys.

He crossed to the port side, lest his uncle should notice the tears which he felt gathering in his eyes, and blinked into the rain at the dim shape of hills to the north. By now they had passed through the narrows into the great inland sea of the Trondheimsfjord, and already the waves were smaller and the wind less gusty. There were other ships, too, most of them heavily laden coasters, herring boats and ferries, though they passed one big ocean-going cargo vessel like their own, heading with square sail toward the mouth of the fjord. Her decks were stacked high with timber.

"An Orkneyman," remarked Thorarin, as she sailed by.

"Shall we see any long ships?" asked Helgi. "Shall we see the ship in which you sailed with King Olaf, Uncle?"

"She will have been made into firewood this long while since, boy," replied Thorarin with a smile. "But as like as not the king's war fleet will be lying at anchor in the roads, and we shall see the long ships well enough."

After two hours' rowing there was a change of watches, and the men who had been breaking their fast with a meal of cold oat porridge washed down with ale now took their turn on the oar benches forward and aft of the cargo space amidships. The *Heron* glided smoothly up the fjord into a light southeasterly wind that was beginning to veer to the south from the deep bay that now opened away to starboard. Thorarin changed course slightly to the east and pointed to the bluff of land that stood out ahead of them on the far side of the bay.

"That headland is called Roaring Ridge," he said. "The town of Nidaros lies beyond it. The town built by King Olaf Tryggvason."

Helgi felt a quickening of the pulse as he thought of the almost legendary viking hero. Some men said that Olaf Tryggvason had not died at the battle of Svold, when he had jumped overboard, fully armed, to escape his enemies. Everyone knew that he could swim like a seal, with or without his heavy coat of mail. Some said that he had been seen years later in a monastery near Jerusalem in the Holy Land. Helgi could see him clearly in his mind from the descriptions of Master Jon of Maddervale: tall, fair-haired and magnificent—the sort of king for whom men gladly laid down their lives.

"Is *this* King Olaf like the other one?" he asked.

Thorarin shrugged his shoulders. "I never met with Olaf Tryggvason," he said. "But from what I have heard, and from what I know of Olaf Haraldsson, his kinsman, I should say that no two men could be less like. The only thing which they have possessed in common is the kingship; that and the Faith, which both have been sworn to defend." He smiled at the expression on Helgi's face, and added, "You will find King Olaf a good and loving master to those that serve him well, Helgi. The other Olaf was a man to die for, maybe; but this is a king to live for and to work for, under God."

Before long, Nidaros came into view, with the wooden spire of a church against the dark green of the hills. They could now see ships anchored in the roads—row after row of slender curved hulls with painted figureheads and shield rails. Helgi stared at them, fascinated, as the *Heron* drew near.

"Uncle," he said suddenly. "Will you tell me again about that viking voyage, when you sailed south with King Olaf, and when the king turned back to Norway?"

"Certainly I will," said Thorarin, pleased. "Seeing these ships at anchor makes it all come back to me as though it had happened yesterday."

And as they picked their way through the channels into Nidaros harbor, Thorarin told his nephew once more about the Viking's Dream.

"It was getting toward midsummer, about ten years past. We had sailed with three ships out of Rouen, in the land that is called Normandy, in the spring; for that was the year after Ethelred, the English king, had been driven out of his realm by Knut the Mighty of Denmark. Olaf Haraldsson was a landless viking at that time. His family was descended from Harald Fairhair, who first claimed the name of king over all Norway; but either they had been made underlings, or were driven out of the land by the Danish kings, and Olaf had followed Ethelred, whom he served for a while, into exile, thinking to win wealth and fame in winning back the English kingdom. But all this came to nothing, as matters turned out; and Olaf was stuck there in Normandy, a pensioner of the earls, Robert and William, which was little to his liking.

"I, Thorarin Nefjolfsson, was in Rouen at that time, also, having traveled south from Iceland with a cargo of skins the summer before, and spent the winter at the earls' court, laying out my gains in such works of art and precious things as I could come by in that land.

"Olaf Haraldsson and I came together, for he was a Norwegian and I an Icelander, and we spoke the same tongue, while many of the Norman chieftains had taken to speaking the Frankish language, which was unknown to us. Olaf was barely a man then, of less than eighteen winters, and I was nigh on twice his age. And besides, he bore a king's name, though he had no kingdom, for his father had been a district king in southern Norway under the Danish Harald Bluetooth. For all this, Olaf was not proud, and we were messmates that winter, so that when spring came, and he looked to find crews to go a-viking, he bade me be one with them.

"What took place on that voyage is of little note, for it went as all viking voyages do, with some fighting and some fleeing and a fair deal of plunder, though King Olaf showed himself to be a skillful captain for his years, and a lucky one. We gained good takings on the coasts of Frankland and Spain, though it seemed to us that our captain was often too mild in his dealings with captured enemies, for he would take no prisoners to be sold for a good price in the northern markets as thralls. Even the heathen people of Spain, who are called Moors and worship the gods Allah and Mahomet, were allowed to go free, for Olaf said that it was not fitting for a Christian man to hold another as his own.

"We came at last to the city of Cadiz, which lies close by the Narrow Sound, the strait between Spain and Africa, the land of the Blue Men.

"Here we sacked the town, after a fierce fight, and won rich treasure from the Moors.

"That night, while the flames from burning houses still lit up the sky, and the bolder people of Cadiz rode up and down the water front, waving their swords and cursing us, we were at anchor out in the harbor, exhausted, most of us, from fighting and drinking. We had destroyed every boat in the town, so that there was little danger of an attack, but nevertheless King Olaf had set watchmen on every ship to guard against surprise. And so we slept on board under the stars. It was too warm in

that southern climate for us to think of pitching the deck
tents; and besides, vikings have to be ready to fight or
man the oars at the first warning.

"So we all slept that night. All, that is, save the watchmen, huddled in their cloaks up on the stern decks, and
maybe a few like myself whose wounds held sleep away
—I had received a slight sword cut on the left thigh—and
also our captain, Olaf Haraldsson.

"I knew that he was awake, for I lay close by him
under one of the stern thwarts. He was leaning against
the starboard gunnel and gazing out across the sea toward the coast of Africa. I saw him shake his head, as if
some thought was troubling him. Then suddenly he
struck the gunnel with his open palm and said aloud, so
that I could hear him, 'That I shall do, whatever may
come of it!' After that he clenched his fist about the hilt
of his sword and whispered, 'I shall sail onward, through
the Narrow Sound, all the way to Jerusalem. My feet shall
touch the Holy Places where my Savior walked.'

"Then he stooped down to enter the small space under
the stern deck that served him as a sleeping quarter, and
I was left alone with my thoughts and with the stars.

"Early the next morning, before dawn, we put out from
Cadiz Bay and anchored a short way along the coast,
where King Olaf called a mast-*thing*, or ships' assembly.
One named Hrani the Far-Traveled, who was the king's
foster father and right-hand man, blew the assembly horn
for the *thing*, and Olaf climbed onto the oar rack at the
foot of the mast to speak, for the three ships were lying
close together.

"The crews crowded aft to hear him, eager to know

what he was going to put before them. They had fared
well on this voyage, and there would be a rich share of
plunder for every man, but most of them hankered after
a cooler climate and a taste of ale beside a northern
fire hearth. Many were landless adventurers, like the king,
but a few had families in Rouen or in England, while
some had followed him all the way from Westland in
Norway.

"'I have summoned this mast-*thing*,' said King Olaf,
'because the time has come for deciding whether we
should go on or turn back; and it is for you, my crews,
to declare your will in this matter, and for me, your captain, to heed your vote, for such is the viking law. But
now I shall tell you what is in my mind. All of you know
what good luck has followed us on this expedition—'

"There was a murmur of assent at this, and one of the
men called out, 'We know that the luck follows you, King
Olaf, and are ready to go with you wherever you decide
to go.'

"There was some argument then, but the king held up
his hand for silence, and continued, 'I will tell you that
this very night past I had made up my mind to sail onward through the Narrow Sound, all the way to Juda-
land and the Holy City of Jerusalem. I have had my
bellyful of pillage and plunder for a while, and would
think of my soul's health, as a Christian, to offer my
sword to Christ, and maybe to serve the emperor at
Micklegarth, that the Greeks call after their chieftain
Constantine.'

"A few of the vikings began to look doubtful and
muttered at this, for there were several heathens among

them, and some of the others were but ill-christianed. But Hrani the Far-Traveled scowled threateningly and lifted his war ax, and Olaf continued.

"'I had made up my mind this night past, as I have told you, before lying down to sleep in Cadiz Harbor. But in the night I had a dream. . . .'

"Nothing could be heard now but the creak of the anchor cables against the ships' sterns as they swung gently in the sea swell. Every man knew that dreams were of great weight in deciding matters of importance, and sometimes could be a guide to things still hidden in the future.

"'My dream was in this manner,' continued the king. 'I thought that, as I lay beneath the stern deck, a man stooped down by me and told me to wake. He was a very tall man, with long, fair hair and beard, and very noble in his bearing and speech; and yet, for a reason that I cannot tell, I was full of fear at his presence. He said to me, "Olaf Haraldsson, put aside this plan of yours, to sail to distant lands. Return to your own land and claim your birthright. For I tell you," he said, "you shall be king of Norway to the end of time."

"'After these words I awoke, and it seemed to me that this had been my kinsman Olaf Tryggvason. And by this token I deem that it is my destiny to be chief king over all Norway, as he was in his time; but that, unlike him, I shall rule many years, and my heirs after me.

"'And so I declare to you that it is now in my mind to turn back, and to sail, with such as will follow me, to Norway.'

"And that," said Thorarin the Shipmaster, "was how King Olaf made up his mind to return to his own land. But now, Helgi, you must be as still as a ptarmigan on a hillside when a fox is near, and not speak a word, for I am about to bring the *Heron* in to the town jetty."

Nidaros

The town of Nidaros lay at the southern end of the Trondheimsfjord, at the mouth of the River Nid, from which it got its name. It was only a few miles west of Hladir, the ancient steading of the powerful earls who had ruled the district in times past, and Olaf Tryggvason had chosen the site both for its harbor and for its strong position, enclosed by water on three sides within the bend of the river and the fjord. Here he had built himself a hall and a church thirty years before, though after his death the place had been abandoned—but for the priest and a few fishermen—until the coming of Olaf Haraldsson, the present king. This Olaf had rebuilt and enlarged the hall and added several new buildings: a courtroom, stores and a guardhouse for the *hird*, or royal bodyguard; and he had made the town his winter capital.

In the spring, about Easter or Pentecost, the court would move south, either to the market town of Tunsberg in the Westfold, which was King Olaf's home country, or to the royal manor at Sarpsborg, near the Swedish frontier. Queen Astrid, who was a Swedish princess by birth, preferred the warmer summers and gentler landscape of the south, and liked to be within visiting distance of her brother, King Onund-Jacob; but King Olaf insisted always that they return about Michaelmas to the Tronderlaw, where the challenge to his authority was greatest and where he could reach out to the unruly and willful chieftains of the north.

Thus, when Thorarin the Icelander docked the *Heron* at the town jetty, he learned that the king and most of the court were still in the south but were expected within a week or two.

Helgi was both disappointed and relieved. Secretly he was beginning to dread the moment when he would give up his freedom to enter the royal service. Still, he was longing to see the king of whom his uncle spoke so warmly.

After seeing to the unloading of his cargo and the

lodging of his crew, Thorarin took the boy with him to the king's garth, a fenced enclosure of buildings that stood some distance from the harbor in the shadow of the tall wooden church.

To Helgi, who had never in his life seen any but low, wooden-gabled buildings of dry stone and turf, the king's hall and the church and all the houses around were of indescribable magnificence and left him speechless with wonder. Beside these the great hall of Gudmund the chieftain at Maddervale, for all its carved and painted beams, was like a stable or cowshed. Here even the meanest outhouse was carved and decorated with paint and gold, and such a wealth of timber was hardly to be found in the whole of Iceland together.

The entrance to the royal garth was guarded by a tall Norwegian in a bearskin jacket. He had a war ax hooked by its blade over his shoulder, and he was leaning against the gateway with his arms folded.

"What men are here?" he asked as they entered the gate, though he did not move.

"Why," answered Thorarin, "it seems to me that your eyesight must be failing you, Calf Arnason, that you do not know an old friend when you see him."

"Thorarin the Icelander, by the rood!" exclaimed the Norwegian, and he dropped his ax to give the merchant a bearlike hug. "Welcome back to Nidaros and to Norway."

"Are your brothers with you?" asked Thorarin. "There are no men I would more gladly see again, unless it be the king himself and Sigvat the Scald."

"In that at least you may be satisfied," replied Calf.

"Your countryman Sigvat is here in Nidaros. My brothers are still with King Olaf in Tunsberg, though."

"What other leading men are here?" asked Thorarin.

"The bishop and his clergy, and a few of the guard, like myself, who came up with Bjorn the Marshal this past week."

"Then Bjorn is not with the king?"

"He is here to make ready for the coming of the court." Calf stooped down from his great height and peered at Helgi. "And what kind of small animal is this that you have with you, Thorarin *minn,*" he said. "Is it yours?"

Thorarin laughed. "He? Oh no. He is my sister's son from Islefirth in the north of Iceland. I have brought him to court to have them make a man of him."

"He's a bit small, isn't he?" said Calf doubtfully. "But if any can make a man of him, I dare take an oath that Bjorn will do it."

The main courtyard of the king's garth was a scene of much activity, with housecarls dashing to and fro on errands in preparation for the king's coming, and with serving wenches chattering and quarreling over their work as they carried out washing, fetched pails of water and sweated under loads of bread and salted meat in the warm sunshine. Nobody had time for Thorarin and Helgi, but at last Thorarin was able to corner and grab hold of a tousle-haired youth with a load of firewood in his arms, whom he refused to release until he told him where Bjorn the Marshal was to be found.

"By your speech, you are Icelanders," said the boy insolently. "What business have you with Master Bjorn?"

Thorarin gave his arm a jerk so that he dropped the wood. "My business is my own, and not for your ears,

Norwegian," he replied sharply. "Let it be enough for
you that I am a friend of King Olaf, and was so before
you were out of your cradle."

At this the boy told them sullenly where Bjorn was to
be found, and they threaded their way between the
buildings, leaving him to pick up his firewood.

"You will find that an Icelander has to stand up for
himself in Norway," said Thorarin. "Even the king's
friendship will not save you from that. Indeed, it will win
you envy."

"What have the Norwegians against us, who are their
kinsfolk?" said Helgi.

Thorarin shrugged his shoulders. "That I cannot say,"
he replied. "But it may be that they grudge us our freedom, because we chose rather to be our own masters, in
the days of King Harald Fairhair, than to bow our heads
to a king."

"And yet you are the friend of King Olaf," Helgi said,
puzzled.

"Maybe the king wearies of too much respect," said
Thorarin with a smile. "Maybe he is glad to have someone about him who will speak his mind without fear."

They found Bjorn the Marshal supervising the dis-
charge of stores in one of the outbuildings. He was a
short, thickset man with fair hair and a red face, and
Helgi thought that he looked bad-tempered. Two or three
traders and a burly, sheepskin-coated farmer, who were
checking the tally of goods as they were brought into the
storehouse, were treating him with much respect. This was
the man who was not only in charge of the royal household,
but also commander of the guard and chief spokesman
for the king himself at *things* and public assemblies. He

was one of the most important men in Norway, and to Helgi it seemed that he intended that none should forget it.

Bjorn nodded to Thorarin without warmth.

"They told me that you were in the town," he said. "You know the king is not yet come. What goods have you to offer? No corn, I suppose, which is what is most needed. Does anything grow on that wind-blasted island of yours?"

Thorarin grinned and shook his head. "I have a few fine fox skins for the king to see," he replied. "But little else, apart from woven cloth and some dried fish. But I scarcely thought to find you playing the steward, Master Bjorn."

Bjorn snorted. "There is no man honest enough, or with sense enough, to deal with these Trondheim rogues," he said. "The steward is sick and his underlings are thieves and swindlers to the very last man. And there are ever men enough who are glad to live off the king's bounty," he added meaningly. "You will find room in the guesthouse."

"Oh, I have business to see to, and will lodge in the town until the king returns," replied Thorarin lightly with a humorous glance at Helgi. "It's about the boy that I wished to speak with you."

Bjorn looked at Helgi with pale blue eyes, as if seeing him for the first time.

"Well?" he asked. "What about him? As you can see, I have small time for talking."

"He is my sister's son, and I have promised to bring him into the king's service," said Thorarin smoothly.

"The devil you did!" exclaimed Bjorn. "He is a foolish

man who promises what is not his own to give. I have turned Norwegian boys of noble birth away; strong and likely youths, at that."

"Helgi is not of noble birth, and he is rather small and not very strong," said Thorarin. "Nevertheless, I think that King Olaf will take him into his service."

Bjorn glared at Thorarin for a moment and his face became redder than ever. Then he turned his back on them without a word and continued to attend to the stores.

"Have no fear, Helgi *minn*," said Thorarin in a whisper, "I'll take you to the master of the pages and he will teach you your duties. Bjorn is not as hard a man as he would have us believe."

That same day Thorarin left the king's garth to attend to his own business, and Helgi, under the guidance of the master of the pages, was swept up in the stream of court life, with so much to learn and to remember that he had no time for a while to be either miserable or homesick. Once or twice he crossed the path of Bjorn, but the marshal pretended not to see him, and his continued presence in the royal household seemed to be taken for granted.

The Norwegian pages were cold and rather hostile at first and left Helgi to himself, but he showed such an eager readiness to do the lowliest tasks that were laid upon him that their manner toward him softened as the days went by. He was befriended, too, by Sigvat, the Icelandic court poet, who often went out of his way to speak a word of encouragement to him.

To a boy who had lived all his life on a small Icelandic farm, where the arrival of a guest had been an event to remember, the bustle and endless coming and going of people at the court was both exciting and confusing. There were district chiefs with quarrels to be settled, merchants with trade goods to sell, common people, farmers and fishermen, with grievances against their landlords, wives of notable men anxious to pay court to the queen, clerics and priests visiting the bishop, great landowners come to pay homage. These were in and out of the royal garth each day, awaiting the king's arrival, or trying to interest some important person in their case, or attending to their business, each according to his or her nature and desires. There were would-be scalds with verses for the king, a soothsayer with predictions about the coming year in Norway, an ambassador from the court of the king of Scotland, a party of Finns from the far north with gifts of reindeer horn and skins and magic charms, a Greenland shipmaster with a rare white falcon to sell, and many others. Helgi was filled with wonder that there should be such a variety of people in the world.

"You wait until the king arrives and starts holding his courts of justice," remarked one of the other pages. "Then it will be twice as busy as it is now, and there will be many more people, to say nothing of all the beggars who will arrive expecting a free meal. The king never turns a poor man away, and every good-for-nothing rogue and vagabond in the country knows as much. Besides that, and all the extra work it means for us pages, we shall have to take turns to attend the king to church at all hours, as well as the daily Mass."

At home in Islefirth, Helgi had lived within a day's ride of the nearest church, so Mass on Sundays and the

chief Holy Days had been the accepted thing in his
family when the weather allowed it. But here in Nidaros,
daily attendance at Mass seemed to be taken for granted,
even among the worldlier members of the court and
bodyguard. This spoke much for King Olaf's influence
over his followers, for if the king was renowned for his
piety and love of the liturgy, it was more that his people
should continue after his example when he was far
away.

One day, about a week after Helgi's arrival at the
king's garth, there was a great stir outside the gateway
just about suppertime, and he learned that the queen had
come, riding overland with an escort of the guard by way
of Gudbrandsdale and the high fells; while the king, it
was said, was now on his way by sea and would arrive
shortly.

Helgi soon had a chance of seeing the queen at close
quarters, for he was sent with another boy to carry hot
water and towels to the bower, to which she went at
once with her maids-in-waiting. This was a small, ornate
building next to the hall. In place of the usual shields
and weapons, its walls were hung with embroidered cloths
and skins, and each room was ablaze with candles in
silver sconces.

Queen Astrid was a tall, pale woman with fair, almost
ash-colored hair and a Swedish lilt to her voice. She was
seated on a couch covered with bearskins, while a maid-
in-waiting pulled off her riding boots. The Icelander,
Sigvat the Scald, stood beside her, talking, as Helgi and
his companion timidly entered her private chamber.

"Put the basin on the chest, boy, and the ewer by it,"
said the queen when she saw them. "No, not like that.

Lay the towel over the ewer to keep the water hot. Where are your wits, boy?"

Helgi fumbled and all but dropped the towel in his confusion, and when he looked up he caught Sigvat's eye.

"Why, if it's not my fellow countryman," said the poet. "This boy is nephew to old Thorarin the Merchant, of whom I spoke."

"Come here, boy," ordered the queen. "What is your name, and how old are you?"

Helgi told her.

"He is young to be away from his mother," said the queen kindly. "Would you like to be in my service, Helgi?"

Helgi felt a hot blush rising to his cheeks, but he replied, "Lady, I would rather serve the king."

Astrid smiled. "That was a frank and manly answer," she said. "You Icelanders have a name for plain speaking, so I might have expected it. You shall serve the king, Helgi, have no fear. But if you could do me a service, too, would you not wish it?"

"Gladly, lady," said Helgi, glancing at Sigvat to see if they were mocking him, but the poet smiled encouragingly.

"I have a foster son who is younger than you, Helgi," said the queen. "His name is Harald, and he is half brother to the king. He is sleeping now, for he has ridden with me from the south and is very weary. His father and mother are both dead. I want you to be a friend to him, Helgi, for you are nearer to him in age than any other here. Will you do that?"

"Yes, lady, I will do that," Helgi replied.

"Good. And you must learn to be patient with him, for he is a child of spirit, and willful and headstrong at times. Master Geir, the German priest, is his tutor, and you shall join with him in his lessons. Where are you sleeping now?"

"In the *stofa*, beside the great hall, with the other pages," answered Helgi.

"Then you shall move your bedding to the guardhouse, where Harald lies."

"In the guardhouse?" said Helgi, surprised.

"Yes, by his own choice he prefers to be with warriors rather than with the womenfolk, and the king has given his leave," explained the queen.

"I will take you there," said Sigvat, "for I sleep there too!"

The guardhouse was like the king's hall, but smaller. It had the same central fire hearth and raised wooden floor, but the two longer walls were divided up into a number of partitions, each containing a shelflike bunk with skins and woven cloth for bedding. In some of the beds men lay sleeping, their shields and weapons hung on the wall beside them. The end gable, too, was entirely covered by racks of spears, bows and war axes, ranged the whole width of the room and as high as a man could reach. Under this, several men sat round a table, playing a game with knucklebones in the flickering light of an oil lamp. Among them Helgi saw Calf Arnason, but the Norwegian gave him no sign of recognition.

Sigvat led him to the end of the room farthest from the door, where a screened and curtained recess filled one corner.

"That is where Bjorn the Marshal sleeps," said the

poet. "If you value your skin, you will try not to disturb him; and keep out of his path early of a morning, too."

In the bunk next to the curtained recess a small boy with flushed cheeks and tousled, corn-colored hair was lying asleep. He muttered and struck out in his sleep, frowning, as Sigvat shifted him gently across to make room for Helgi.

"You'll be glad of the warmth when the cold nights come," said Sigvat, "but it will not surprise me if you find Harald an uneasy bedfellow."

The next morning Helgi awoke to a violent blow in the chest that made him sit up sharply. The other boy was sitting beside him, frowning.

"Who are you, and what are you doing here?" asked Harald. "I'll get my brother the king to have you beaten."

"I'm Helgi, and your mother said that I was to come," answered Helgi. "I mean the queen," he added, remembering that Harald had no mother or father. "I'm an Icelander, and I have to be your friend."

"I choose my own friends," said Harald, "and I won't have an Icelander sharing my bed. They smell of fish. Bjorn the Marshal says so."

"Say that again and I'll hit you, and I don't care if the king is your brother," said Helgi, furious.

"Icelanders smell of fish."

The next moment the cramped space was a tangle of wildly waving arms and legs, and the wooden partition thudded and shook behind them. Although he was the elder by two years, Helgi was not having it all his own way. Harald fought with a fierce, demonic rage that seemed to give him double strength, and soon Helgi found himself rolled onto the floor with the younger boy

on top of him. He struggled to throw him off and get to
his feet, and had just succeeded in this when a blow
from behind sent him flying. At the same instant he saw
Harald spin round like a top and go sprawling in the
other direction.

"Is this place to be turned into a nursery of squabbling
brats, so that a man may no longer sleep in peace?" an
angry voice demanded.

Helgi turned and saw Bjorn the Marshal standing
above them, his face purple with fury. He was clad only
in his undershirt and linen hose, and his hair and beard
were awry.

"I'll teach you brats to disturb my sleep," he bellowed,
and then Helgi saw that he was holding a leather belt
in his hand. . . .

For days after, Helgi and Harald showed great care
when they sat down, and both of them seemed to have a
rather unmanly preference for cushions and other soft
surfaces. But sometimes when they looked at Bjorn the
Marshal and then at each other they would smile, and
from that time they were firm friends, though they often
quarreled.

Helgi soon found that he enjoyed several advantages
from his friendship with Harald. In the first place he was
free of many of the morning tasks, such as cleaning out
the great hall and polishing weapons and attending to
the horses in the stables, for these were carried out by
the other pages at the time when he was closeted with
Harald and Master Geir the priest, stumbling through
the Latin letters and learning about the lives of holy men
in other lands.

Harald was impatient and contemptuous of such learning, although he was careful to hide his feelings from
Master Geir, who was a strict disciplinarian and a be-
liever in the rod. But to Helgi he would speak his mind
freely.

"One day I shall be a king, like my brother," he said.
"What has a king to do with prayers and penances and
Latin books? He must be a warrior, fearless and skilled
in battle, and a scourge to his enemies. Bjorn the Marshal
says so, and in this he is right."

"But your brother King Olaf believes in prayers and
penances and in the learning of priests," said Helgi.

Harald shrugged his shoulders. "He is like my father,
whom men called Sigurd Sow," he replied. "He was a
king, but he thought only of his crops and his barns.
Bjorn says that I am like my mother. She was King Olaf's
mother, too, but Bjorn says that I have more of her spirit
than he has. I shall be a great king and conquer new
lands for Norway."

Helgi quite enjoyed his lessons with Master Geir, although he did not say so to Harald. He was a slow
learner and came in for his share of blows and rebukes
from the strict priest, but once he had mastered a thing,
though it took time, he seldom forgot it.

His progress in the arts of war, which they learned
with the other pages under Bjorn himself, was less satisfactory. He was a fair horseman and a good shot—
though he could not handle the full-sized bow like some
of the older boys—but his swordplay and ax play were
feeble. Bjorn drove him without mercy, making him practice with a heavy sword until his arm was aching with

weariness, and telling him that he would do better stirring porridge in the king's kitchen.

Helgi's favorite times, though, were the hours which he and Harald spent with Sigvat the Scald, learning the rudiments of the noble art of verse-making. Harald was good at this.

"When I first came to court, King Olaf refused to listen to the verses which I had made in his honor," Sigvat told them one day. "He said that such arts were for heathen men, with their tales of the old gods and goddesses. But I persuaded him to hear me, and since then he has become a scald himself. It is a craft that kings should not despise."

"When I am a king, I shall have my own scalds to do my verse-making," declared Harald. Nevertheless, he listened with interest when Sigvat recited to them the old lays of gods and heroes which had been handed down from past ages.

One of his special favorites was the lay that told how the mighty god Thor, son of Odin, went fishing with the giant Hymir, using the head of an ox as bait, and how he hooked the World-Serpent that girdles the whole earth.

Swiftly the swain to the woods he went,
an ox all black there stood before him.
The bane of giants then broke from the bull
its high hill of double horns.

The goats' master now bade the boatman
steer the steed of the slipway further;
though the giant then declared
little his longing to row longer.

Alone, on his hook did moody Hymir
draw to the top two whales together;
but aft in the stern the son of Odin
artfully fashioned himself a line.

The defender of men, the dragon-slayer,
on his hook he hung the head of the bull.
Gaped at the bait the gods' hater,
the girdle of all the Earth below.

Daringly drew Thor the doughty
that venomous serpent up from the deep.
With his hammer aloft the hill of hair
of the wolf's bond brother loathsome he smote.

Helgi enjoyed hearing the old verses, too. But he was
more interested to hear of their own times, especially
of events in other lands which Sigvat had visited, for,
like Thorarin, Sigvat was a great traveler, but had more
skill in describing what he had seen.

Helgi repeated to him Thorarin's story of the viking
raid on Cadiz and asked if he had been with King Olaf
in those days. The poet shook his head and said that
his father Thord, who was also a scald, had been with
the king when he returned to Norway and had told
him about it.

"Tell us," said Harald, though he had heard the story
many times before. He was ever eager to hear of ad-
ventures and battles, whether of today or of long ago.

"Yes, tell us," agreed Helgi, and Sigvat, who was in a
good mood that day, allowed himself to be persuaded.

So he told them the story of the Coming of the King
to Norway.

"The same autumn that he dreamed his dream, King Olaf sailed back to Normandy with his fleet, and he spent much time in the winter getting such intelligence as he could of events in Norway. At this time Earl Eric was the chief man in the land, holding it first under King Svein Forkbeard of Denmark, who had fought beside him against Olaf Tryggvason, and then later under King Knut the Mighty, son of Svein. King Knut was then busy strengthening his grip on the new kingdom that he had won for himself in England, and he had little enough time to think of his own land of Denmark, to say nothing of a poor, distant colony in Norway. But Earl Eric had power to command only in his own country, the Tronder-law, which is what the Norwegians call these parts bordering on Trondheimsfjord. Beyond that, the land had gone back to the rule of the chiefs and the folk kings, much as it had been before the time of Olaf Tryggvason. And, what was more, most of the people had slipped back into the heathen ways of their forefathers.

"The following spring, in order not to break faith with the sons of Ethelred the English, King Olaf led his ships against King Knut and fought several battles in England. But his mind was still on Norway, and when he heard that Earl Eric was out of the country for the while, he at once laid up his long ships in a secret harbor, in the place called Northumberland, and bought two merchant vessels with part of the great horde of gold which he had amassed on his viking voyages. Then he picked from his crews one hundred and twenty men, the bravest and best, all well armed and sworn to serve him faithfully to death. With these alone, he said, he would win Norway.

"The two merchant ships passed unnoticed through the Norwegian skerries to an island off the west coast. Their sails were bleached by sea salt, and much repaired, and there were other signs to show that they had taken a hard beating from the wind and the waves before reaching this safe anchorage.

"Olaf and his men landed in a small creek on the northern side of the island, under steep cliffs of red rock. The king turned to Hrani, his foster father, who was at his side, and asked what place this was.

"'This is the island of Selja, lord,' replied Hrani, naming the place which was linked in the minds of all Christian Norwegians with certain holy Irish hermits who had died there nearly a century before.

"'That should be a token of good luck,' said Olaf with a smile. 'Now, let no man go ashore in front of me.'

"The men on board the two vessels watched expectantly as their young leader slipped over the gunnel and began to wade up the beach. Hrani followed close behind him.

"A small stream ran out into the sea just above the point where the ships had anchored, and the foreshore was soft and muddy. As Olaf stepped onto what he took to be dry ground, his foot sank in the mud and he stumbled, falling on one knee.

"'Now I fell, Hrani,' he said.

"'You did not fall, my king,' replied Hrani. 'You set your foot firmly in Norwegian ground.'

"Olaf smiled rather ruefully as he stood up and wiped the mud off his hose. 'It may be so,' he said, 'if God wills it.'

"They stayed on Selja only long enough to take on

water and some fresh meat, which they bought from a farmer on the island, but Olaf would not leave before he had visited the little shrine built by King Olaf Tryggvason high up on the mountainside by the cave of the holy hermits, and heard Mass said by the priest who was its guardian.

"Less than an hour later, the two ships had gone on their way to the south, leaving the island to the sea birds and the sheep, with little to mark their visit but a half-obliterated footprint on the shore.

"But the men who followed King Olaf were soon saying that his luck had not left him, for, within a few days of this, by the merest chance and almost without bloodshed, Hakon, the son of Earl Eric, his chief enemy, had fallen into Olaf's hands while sailing, unsuspecting, along the coast from the south.

"Hakon Ericsson was no more than a child at this time, and Olaf himself was but at the threshold of manhood; and yet men said that there were never two men so unlike.

"Hakon had inherited the good looks of the earls of Hladir: he was tall for his age and fair, with long hair like silk held about his head by a golden band. The king, on the other hand, was short and stocky, his hair and beard an indeterminate reddish brown and cut short like a peasant's. Only his eyes were unforgettable: clear and piercing like a sharp sword.

"The young Earl Hakon was led in bonds to the king's ship and he stood in silence before Olaf.

"'Men do not lie when they say that you are a handsome family,' said the king, 'but it looks as if your luck has left you now.'

"The boy answered boldly. 'That was not a question of luck. You caught us off our guard. Besides, I have had little practice in war. Others of my kin have got the better of their enemies before this, and it may be that the next time we meet, things will not go so well for you.'

"Olaf looked at the boy almost with pity in his eyes and said, 'Has it not entered your mind, Earl Hakon, that from now on you may not be able either to win or lose?'

"The young earl passed his tongue over his lips and then, looking the king straight in the eyes, said, 'it is in your power to decide that.'

"'What will you do if I let you go, whole and unharmed?' asked Olaf suddenly.

"'What do you ask?' said Hakon slowly, clutching at the hope that was offered, and yet not daring to believe in it. 'What is your condition, King Olaf?'

"'That you should leave Norway at once and renounce all your rights, and take an oath never to fight against me again.'

"Earl Hakon took this oath, and the king allowed him and his men to go in peace; but there were some among Olaf's followers who grumbled at this act of mercy, and said that he would have cause to regret it later.

"After this, King Olaf sailed east with his men into the Oslofjord, where he knew that his strongest following was to be found, for it was his own country.

"News of his coming was brought to his mother, Queen Asta, in Westfold, where she lived with his stepfather, a small folk king in those parts," continued Sigvat. "This man, King Sigurd Sow, your father, Harald, was a great farmer, and he was out working in the fields when the news arrived. Queen Asta at once prepared the house for her son's coming, and she sent messengers to her husband, King Sigurd, with his robes of state and his best riding horse. The messengers told him that his stepson, Olaf Haraldsson, was come back from the south, and it was the queen's wish that he should be received in a fitting manner.

"King Sigurd smiled and said that it was just like Asta.

"'This is great news,' he added, 'but I can see that those who will risk their life and land for this Olaf will be in danger of losing both; for he is setting himself up against powerful odds, and is likely to bring down upon himself the wrath of King Knut of Denmark.'

"Nevertheless, King Sigurd put on his robes of state there in the cornfield: goatskin hose, with gilded spurs on his feet and a tunic of satin cloth with a scarlet cloak over it. And he girded himself with a richly ornamented sword and put a gilded helm on his head, and he rode in from the fields with about thirty men to receive Olaf.

"When he drew near the homestead he could see King Olaf's standard above the turf roofs of the buildings. There were more than a hundred armed men about it in the yard, and King Sigurd rode forward to greet his stepson, and bade him drink with him in the hall.

"Then Queen Asta came out from the carved and painted doorway and kissed her son, and told him that all they had, both of land and men, were his for the holding. And she led him into the hall to the high seat, and a great feast was held in his honor.

"Soon after that King Sigurd called together all the folk kings of the Uplands and persuaded them to accept

Olaf as the rightful heir of Harald Fairhair and chief king of all Norway. And a *thing*, or assembly of the people, was summoned; and the small farmers and the common people gladly acclaimed King Olaf, for they were sick of the tyranny of King Knut's underlings and the lawlessness of the great chieftains. But King Sigurd Sow remarked, 'The common people are ever ready for something new. It was so when Olaf Tryggvason seized power, but you know how short a time he reigned.'

"At this, Queen Asta said to her son, 'As for me, I would rather that you reigned a short time like Olaf Tryggvason, who was king of all Norway, than that you died of old age and were never more of a king than my husband, Sigurd Sow.'"

"It is true," said Harald when Sigvat had finished. "My father was very wise, but men say that he had little spirit for a king. Everyone tells me that I take after my mother, Queen Asta."

"Was King Olaf accepted by everyone after that?" asked Helgi.

Sigvat the Scald shook his head.

"The powerful landowners of Norway were, for the most part, against him, even then," he said. "Erling Skjalgsson, for one, whom men call the 'king of Rogaland,' for he rules there in the west like a king; and Thorir Hound, who is chief over the northlands, in Halogaland and beyond to the borders of Finnmark; and, of course, the earls of Hladir, who had ruled in Trondheim."

"But you said that Earl Eric was out of the country, and that his son Hakon took an oath to leave Norway and never to fight against King Olaf again," said Helgi.

"What I said was true, boy," answered Sigvat. "Earl Eric was in England, helping his master Knut to hold his kingdom against the English. What is more, about this time, the earl died of a sickness, though some men say that the doctor who attended him was one who had served with Olaf Tryggvason against him at Svold. But Earl Eric had a brother, Svein, who held lands under the Swedish king in the south of Norway. This Svein gathered together a mighty fleet and he and Erling and others attacked King Olaf down in the south. About this time, I was come from Iceland to be with my father, and I sailed with the king on his ship, the *Carlshead*."

"Tell us about the battle," said Harald eagerly. But Sigvat shook his head.

"I made a ballad about it," he replied shortly. "We overcame the earl's ships, and he fled eastward to Sweden. He died soon after in the Swedish lands across the sea, Holmgarth of the Russians"

He smiled, as if diverted by his own memories, and added, "It was my first sea fight. I remember it as though it was yesterday.

> " 'Tis in my mind that many
>   Of them that came from Trondheim's
>   Firth returned not north
>   Again, from our fight with Svein.
>   Many gold-wearing warriors
>   Brave there were, that their wave steeds
>   Forsook in the battle and sank,
>   Dead, to the sea's bed!"

There was a silence when Sigvat ended, and then he patted Harald on the shoulder.

"Sometime I will tell you all about it, boy," he said. "But not now, for the mood is not on me."

"After that battle, was King Olaf acknowledged by all in Norway?" asked Helgi.

"Acknowledged? Ay, that he was, and proclaimed with weapon-take at every *thing* up and down the land. But he had his enemies, Helgi," said Sigvat, "and still has, among the rich and powerful, and those that love not the new ways. For he set his mind firmly on one thing from the start: that this land of Norway shall turn wholly from heathendom and follow the Faith of Christ."

King Olaf

A few days after this, when Helgi was in the guardhouse cleaning weapons for the men who were to go on duty that evening, Thorarin the Icelander came in with Sigvat.

"Your uncle says that the king's fleet has been sighted off Agdaness," the scald told him. "It will not be long now before it arrives."

Helgi, who had been waiting so impatiently for this moment, now felt a shiver of apprehension run through him.

"What manner of man is the king?" he asked.

Sigvat laughed dryly and inquired whether Thorarin had not spoken often enough about him. "He has known King Olaf longer than any, save perhaps Bjorn the Marshal," he said. "Have you told the boy of your meeting with the king when you first came to Nidaros, Thorarin *minn?*"

The merchant grinned and shook his head. "Do you want me to lose the respect of my kinsfolk?" he said. "Still, I'll tell him, so that he may see that the king is a merry companion and a true man, whatever others may say of him."

"Why, what do others say of him?" asked Helgi, but Sigvat silenced him with a frown.

"I suppose the truth is that I must have in me something of the court fool," began Thorarin, smiling. "For the most part, this is a role that is played by the king's scalds," he added with a comic leer at the poet, "but it seems that Sigvat here is of too sad and sour a nature for that."

"I have seen such beings in England and at the court of the earls in Rouen," said Sigvat. "They are men of low birth and breeding and I would not take it well to be compared with them."

"I do not claim high birth, either," said Thorarin. "And it may be that I have this other thing in common with such men, and that is that I dare to speak my mind plainly to the king."

"It is true," said Sigvat. "He is the only man I know

who dares do that at all times, Helgi, and I am willing to admit it."

"The king has gathered many sorts of men about him," continued Thorarin. "Some are clever, like Sigvat; some brave, like Bjorn; some handsome to look at, like the Arnason brothers; some holy, like the bishop or Master Geir. I think that I am the only man he has chosen for ugliness."

"You are joking, Uncle," said Helgi, but Thorarin shook his head. "The first time I met King Olaf, after he returned to Norway," he said, "he let me sleep in his chamber, in the bunk opposite his own. When he awoke in the morning, it seems that he saw one of my feet sticking out from beneath the bedclothes." Stretching out a foot, Thorarin gazed at it ruefully. It was a very large foot on the end of a long, thin shank, and even inside its leathern calfskin boot it looked grotesque and comic. Helgi tried his hardest not to smile.

Thorarin looked at him and winked. "The king saw my foot, as I have told you, and, seeing that I was awake then, he said to me, 'I wager that there is not a foot uglier than that in all the town.' 'I take your wager, lord,' I said. 'I'll find another foot in the town uglier than this one.' 'Very well,' he said, 'whichever one of us wins shall demand what he will of the other.' 'Then I have won the wager, lord,' I said, 'for here is a foot uglier than the one you have seen.' And with that I took my other foot from under the bedclothes and showed it to him. 'The first was ugly with five toes on it; but this has a toe missing.' But do you think that the king would accept defeat? Not Olaf. He said, 'The first had five ugly toes, and this one only four. I have won the wager,' and he laughed and laughed, until every man in the house was awake."

"And did you have to pay the wager, Uncle?" asked Helgi. "Did the king demand something of you?"

"I have heard that he did," said Sigvat. "Was it not then at his request that you took the old Upland king, Hrærek, out of Norway and kept him in Iceland until his death?"

"The old king who had his eyes put out?" asked Helgi. "I saw him when I was small. My mother told me that he was happy in his last years at Calfskin. But it was a cruel thing to blind him."

"Who are you to judge, boy?" said Sigvat sternly. "That man plotted time after time against the king's life, and yet he spared him. You asked what manner of man King Olaf was. Well, I shall tell you. He is a great prince and a wise ruler. There is none like him in all the north. But if he has a fault, it is that he pays too much heed to priests and clerks, and his judgment is sometimes clouded by their counsel."

"Speak not so to the boy," said Thorarin, frowning and glancing about him; then he held up his hand.

"Listen," he said. "Do you hear that? I think that soon Helgi will be able to find out for himself what manner of man King Olaf is."

There was a noise of distant shouting outside and the blowing of a horn, and just then the bell of St. Clement's church began to ring.

"The king!" exclaimed Sigvat. "He has arrived."

People were streaming along the muddy street outside the royal garth, all moving toward the harbor to see the

king's fleet sail in. Helgi saw Harald in front of him and
ran fast to catch up.

"Who said you . . . could come out, Helgi?" panted
Harald angrily. "You are supposed to be . . . at call . . .
in the guardhouse . . . till supper. I'll tell Bjorn . . . and
you . . . will be punished."

"What about you?" said Helgi. "Bjorn gave the same
order to us both."

"The king's my brother . . . and you're not to speak to
me like that."

"I'll try to remember," Helgi called back over his shoulder as he left the younger boy behind.

"Come back! Wait! Helgi, wait for me."

Helgi smiled to himself as he dodged through the
crowd. *Let Harald call; I'm not his servant,* he thought.
He was filled with a feverish excitement and ran as fast
as he could to be among the first at the jetty. But there
was already a crowd waiting there when he arrived, and
he had to push his way and climb up onto a wooden
mooring post to see over the heads in front.

Three great long ships were gliding up the fjord in the
clear sunshine. Their sails were furled and the oars
flashed together under the rows of painted shields like
the legs of long, striped insects creeping over the smooth
water.

The leading vessel was already past the outer mark-
ing buoy, and Helgi could see that its graceful, curved
stem was crowned by a figurehead in the shape of a man's
head.

"That's her. That's the *Carlshead,*" shouted somebody
below him. "Long live King Olaf!" And the shout was

taken up by the crowd. "Long live King Olaf! God bless the king!"

A small group of men could now be seen standing in the stern of the ship beside the steering oar. One, taller than the rest and clad in a scarlet cloak, seemed to be giving orders, and Helgi was certain that he must be the king. The rowers shipped their oars and the *Carlshead* glided in toward the jetty. Some of the palace guard pushed forward from behind Helgi to clear a way through the crowd. He saw Bjorn among them, with Harald close behind, and clung fast to his post, hoping not to be seen. But the eyes of all were on the ship.

Ropes were thrown ashore and the *Carlshead* bumped gently against the jetty. A moment later a gangplank had been pushed out from the stern.

But it was not the tall man in scarlet who stepped ashore first. It was a short, rather heavy figure in blue.

"King Olaf! God bless King Olaf!" shouted the crowd, and the short man waved in acknowledgment with one hand as he steadied himself with the other on the arm of Bjorn the Marshal.

Helgi felt a bitter pang of disappointment.

Was this the man who had conquered Norway and seized for himself the crown of Olaf Tryggvason, that magnificent hero of Icelandic storytellers? The king whom Sigvat had praised so highly? This short, stout man with reddish-brown hair and a wispy beard, who looked more like a trader or a priest than a warrior? Now Helgi understood why his enemies called him Olaf the Fat.

The king moved off with rather an ungainly walk through the passage which Bjorn's men had cleared for him. The man in scarlet and several others went after him, laughing and talking among themselves. Then the crowd closed in and streamed along behind toward the royal garth.

Helgi followed with a heavy heart.

The first few days after the king's arrival, Helgi saw him only at a distance, surrounded by court officials or members of the bodyguard, on his way to Mass or to the hall of justice. Besides, the master of the pages and Bjorn the Marshal between them saw to it that both Helgi and Harald were too fully occupied to find time for hanging about and staring. Even in church the king was only a dim figure standing or kneeling up near the altar, while the pages crowded at the back near the door.

Then one day a message was brought to the guard-house. Harald was to attend his half brother to Vespers that evening and wait on him at table, and his Icelandic companion might accompany him. The messenger, who was one of the queen's servants, told them that they were to present themselves, washed and decently clad, to the steward at the great hall, on the stroke of the bell for Nones.

About two hours later they were both standing in the church less than a yard from King Olaf in the flickering candlelight, while the voices of the choir rose and echoed in the wooden roof and the bishop sat with his clergy in the apse behind the high altar, like the images of the saints on the walls.

The king was dressed in black with a cloak and hood of gray fur hanging from his shoulders, and he had a gold chain about his neck and a thin band of gold round his head. He was standing very still, his head bowed slightly forward, listening to the singing of the psalms. When they came to the Gloria Patri, and the bishop and priests stood and bowed toward the altar, Bjorn the Marshal, who was standing beside the king, turned and nodded to Harald. The boy at once stepped forward with a cushion that he was holding, but the king motioned him away with a gesture and knelt on the floor.

Afterwards, at supper, there were some envious glances from the older pages as Helgi and Harald took up their places on either side of the king's high seat, with the steward close behind. On the right of the king sat the bishop and court chaplains, including Master Geir, the boys' tutor. On the left were counselors of state and men of note, among them Calf Arnason, who had lately been appointed the king's governor in Trondheim. Opposite, on the far side of the long fire, at another table, Bjorn the Marshal sat in the seat of honor, with members of the guard and officials of the royal household. These included Sigvat the Scald and Thorarin among their number. Thorarin had earned himself a much-coveted place in the ranks of the bodyguard by his services to the king years ago, and was still entitled to claim the privileges of a guardsman. Sitting between him and Sigvat there was another, younger man whom Helgi had not seen before.

There was little talk at table until men had satisfied their hunger. Then, after the meat troughs and platters had been carried away, the king washed his hands from a basin held by Harald and wiped them on a clean towel. After that he nodded to the steward, who rapped on the wooden floor with his staff of office, and the servingmen and pages stepped forward with pitchers of mead and ale to fill the drinking horns.

The king and chief men and all the more important guests were served with Frankish wine out of gold and silver vessels. The steward himself filled the king's goblet, then handed the golden ewer to Helgi, who clutched it nervously, watching to see when more would be needed.

The king struck the board with the handle of his dagger for silence and gave a toast in honor of Christ and His Blessed Mother. After that the bishop raised his cup for the saints Michael and Clement, and for the Holy Sunniva and her companions who had died on the island of Selja.

"May their prayers and their example inspire us to the winning of Norway for God and His Church," he said, "and to the overthrow of the heathen devils, Thor and Odin, and all their worshipers." He spoke with a strange accent, for, like most of the priests then in Norway, Bishop Grimkel was an Englishman.

After the toasts, ale, wine and mead flowed freely for since the queen and her ladies were not present—they dined in the great hall only on special occasions—there was no stinting of hospitality. Nevertheless, the king drank sparingly and Helgi's ewer was seldom needed. Once, when he was pouring, the king looked up, and Helgi found himself gazing into the most penetrating pair of gray-blue eyes he had ever seen. In his confusion he spilled some of the wine on the table and got cuffed by the steward for his pains, but he scarcely noticed the blow.

There was much talk over the drinking.

The bishop spoke of the state of the Church in the

north of Norway. In Trondheim and the neighboring
country, he said, men went to Mass on Sundays and holy
days; but they still practiced every kind of heathen super-
stition on the quiet, for luck and for good harvests. As
for the folk of Halogaland and the far north, it was
known that the old heathen feasts were kept up quite
openly by the chieftains and attended by everyone.

"In this they show defiance both for the laws of God
and for the king's edict," said the bishop, and all the
clerks by him nodded their heads in agreement.

"The Halogalanders have ever been a proud, willful
people," said a red-faced chieftain, sitting to the left of
the counselors, "and to my mind the worst among them
is Thorir Hound himself, the king's liegeman and landholder. In temper he is too much like his noble kinsman,
Erling of Rogaland."

Calf Arnason now spoke. He was seated between two
men who were so like him in features that Helgi knew
them to be his brothers, Finn and Thorberg. The three
were known throughout Norway for their strength and
their good looks.

"I must answer for the people of Trondheim," said
Calf. "This summer the harvest has been bad, and men
are slow to change their ways. The customs which they
have learned from their fathers are not easily forgotten,
and I think that there is little harm in them. As for
Thorir Hound, the king would be wise to let him run
awhile, and not hold him on a short leash—"

"The customs of the heathen are blasphemous and call
down the wrath of God," cried Master Geir. "It is on
such—the old wives' tales and sorcery of the peasants—

that the bad harvest is to be blamed. And, still more, the first-fruit and Yule feasts of the chieftains—"

"An unruly hound must be whipped to heel," shouted Bjorn the Marshal, striking the table with his ale horn.

The king raised his hand and there was a silence.

"And what do you say, Sigvat the Icelander?" he asked.

The poet shrugged his shoulders. "In my country such feasts are held by those of the old belief, and men think little of it. But, touching the chieftains of Halogaland and their loyalty to you, lord, there is a way to test it. For the winter-nights' feast, and that at Yuletide and in the spring, much corn and malt are needed. This has been a hard summer, and if corn is short in the south and here in Trondheim, then how much more so will it be in Halogaland. If the king were to make a decree, forbidding the shipment of corn from one district to another . . ."

"By the saints, you are right, Sigvat," said the king.

"Trust an Icelander to think of something clever," Bjorn was heard to mutter. "From a land of foxes come a fox's wiles."

"Is it our fault if King Harald Fairhair drove all the brains out of Norway and into Iceland, more than a hundred years past?" asked Sigvat smoothly, and there was an appreciative laugh from the Norwegians.

"Better not bandy words with Sigvat," the king called to Bjorn. "You'll be sure to get the worst of it. Besides, he has a fellow scald from his own country beside him to back him up."

Eyes were turned toward the young man sitting between Sigvat and Thorarin at the marshal's table.

"Who is that?" whispered Helgi to Harald.

"His name is Thormod, that's all I know," replied Harald. "He is an Icelander and a poet. But then, all Icelanders are poets, aren't they?"

"I'm not," said Helgi. "Nor is my uncle Thorarin."

"Will you two stop twittering like a nest of sparrows behind me," a loud voice boomed at them suddenly, and they saw the king glaring back at them over his shoulder. "I know my kinsman Harald, but who is the other?"

Helgi was struck dumb with fright; then he saw that under the bushy, reddish eyebrows the piercing eyes had a kindly twinkle in them.

"Well, boy, what's your name? You, come over here."

The steward bustled forward, fussing. "Lord, the boy is a playmate of your brother's. He is an Icelandic boy. . . . It was the queen's order, but if Your Highness pleases—"

"I told the boy to come here, not you," snapped the king. "Go away!"

The steward skipped back hastily and pushed Helgi up to the table.

"So you are the boy of whom Thorarin the Merchant has spoken to me, are you?" said the king. "Well, has Odin's raven pecked out your tongue? I asked your name."

"Helgi, lord," said Helgi, finding his voice.

"It is a good name," said the king. "Helgi means 'holy.' Are you a good boy, Helgi?"

"I . . . I don't know," answered Helgi.

"Do you say your prayers morning and evening and go to Mass regularly? But then, your confessor has asked

you these questions. Your countrymen are sometimes
weak in their faith"—the king glanced across at Sigvat,
who was now deep in conversation with Thormod—"but
I trust you will always hold fast to the teaching of our
Holy Mother the Church. Why have you come to Norway, boy? You are young to be away from your mother,"
he added.

"I have come to serve you, lord," replied Helgi.

"Then be a good friend to my brother Harald," said
the king. "I think I can see that you are a good boy and
gentle of spirit. Teach Harald gentleness, and you will
have served him, and me, well."

When the boys went to bed that evening, Helgi said,
"I like King Olaf. I know now that he is good and
kind."

"You have seen only the one side of him," replied
Harald. "All that talk about gentleness. You should see
him when he is in a rage. Even Bjorn the Marshal and
Sigvat are afraid of him then."

There were no lessons for the boys on the following
day, for the king was riding out to meet with the farmers
of the neighboring district, and most of the court was to
ride with him, including Master Geir, his private chaplain. Instead, all the pages were sent to the stables to
help the grooms get ready all the horses for this caval-
cade.

Helgi enjoyed stable work, for it reminded him of
home, with the strong horse smell and animal warmth
and the noise of hoofs and heavy breathing in an enclosed space. He might have been in the stable or the
cowhouse back in Islefirth, helping his father to muck
out the stalls or carry hay. But he hated the grooms here

in the king's stables; they were of a surly, malicious disposition and would take it out on the boys if they had a chance. Only Harald was safe from their malice, because of his close relationship to the king, and him they treated with a fawning deference that Helgi found hard to stomach. He spoke of this once to Sigvat, who told him that the men were for the most part thralls from the west—from Ireland and the Scottish isles—taken in war or sold to Norwegian traders in the northern markets.

"Such men have a bitterness in themselves that dies hard, no less when they are well housed and fed in a king's garth," he said.

This morning tempers seemed more than usually frayed. Bjorn the Marshal was not in the best of moods after a night's heavy drinking and an early rise to attend the king at Mass. His face was redder than usual and his eyes bloodshot, and he passed his ill humor on to the head groom, who in turn passed his on to the stable thralls.

One of the king's favorite riding horses was a gray stallion from Sweden. This was a mettlesome creature that had been shut in the stables these past few days and corn-fed against the time when he would be needed by his master. After roaming the meadows about Nidaros all the summer through with his mares, the stallion found this loss of freedom irksome, and so he was wild and unmanageable when they led him out to be saddled.

Helgi kept well clear of the prancing hoofs, but one of the thralls was kicked and bowled over. The man leaped to his feet, not badly hurt but in a furious rage. He picked up the whip that had fallen from his hand and struck the horse across the nose, so that it whinnied and reared up.

Just then the king came into the yard and saw what was happening.

With half a dozen strides he crossed over to where the man was standing and, without a pause, struck him in the face and sent him flying.

"Dog of a thrall," he shouted, "do you lift your hand to my Grani?"

The groom cowered on the ground with an arm raised to ward off further blows. His face was contorted with a mixture of fear and malice, and Helgi heard him snarl, "If I were King Olaf's beast, I would not be treated so."

The king's face went white and then red, and his eyes blazed. Without a word he picked up the whip that was lying on the ground before him and began to beat the man, fiercely and silently. All that could be heard was the sound of the blows and the king's heavy breathing.

Bjorn the Marshal came running up.

"What has the man done, lord?" he asked. "Shall I order the guard to take him and put him to death?" At his gesture, two men of the bodyguard ran forward and would have seized the thrall, but that the king's blows prevented them. Then he dropped the whip and, seeing them, motioned them away.

"Let the man go," he said wearily. "I am to blame." Then he added, "I shall not ride out today. See that the horses are put back in the stables."

Afterwards Harald said, with something like admiration in his voice, "My brother Olaf has a *berserk* rage at times. I'm not afraid of him, of course, but everybody else is—or nearly everybody."

That evening, though, it was Helgi's duty to attend the king after supper until he retired to bed.

After the tables had been cleared away, King Olaf left the great hall to go to Compline. Only a handful of courtiers and a single guard walked with him across the dark and deserted streets to St. Clement's. Helgi knelt with the others near the back of the church, while the king said his night prayers before the high altar. He had been ordered not to let the king out of his sight until he was dismissed.

For a long time after the last echo of plain chant had died away and the clergy left the choir, the king remained kneeling, a bowed figure in the flickering candle-light. All the courtiers went out of the church, until only Helgi and the guard were left.

The king seemed to be leaning against one of the wooden pillars at the entrance to the choir. He was so still that Helgi thought he might have fallen asleep at his prayers and, greatly daring, the boy tiptoed nearer. Still the king did not move, and at last Helgi plucked up courage to go beside him and glance into his face. His eyes were closed, but tears were running down his cheeks and his lips were moving as though in prayer. Helgi held his breath, fearing to disturb him.

Suddenly the king spoke aloud, and Helgi started back in alarm. But the king's were not for him.

"Have mercy upon me, Christ, and give me strength," he said, "that I may overcome this devil that torments me."

Soon after this he stood up and, seeing Helgi there, said to him, "Boy, it is time you were abed."

Helgi's choice as special page and companion to the

king's young brother had not passed unnoticed, and it earned him some envy and hard words from his former messmates. One of the older pages, a lanky Norwegian youth named Hauk, took particular pleasure in showing his malice, calling Helgi a whey-faced pudding-eater, an Icelandic cod's head and a queen's pet. Helgi was not thin-skinned, though; he had been called worse names in his time by the boatswain of the *Heron*. He shrugged off the offensive remarks and even returned them in kind, calling Hauk a long-legged Norwegian troll and a heathen eater of horse meat. In this way he earned a number of furtive cuffs, but he enjoyed a certain security in being so young, for he knew that this protected him from harsher treatment. In the end, he even won a kind of amused toleration from the older boys, who would abuse him for the pleasure of hearing his quick and biting answers.

"The tongue of an Icelander is dipped in acid," they would say, laughing.

Harald, who was quick-tempered and impulsive and also, according to Sigvat, had the makings of a good poet, was, nevertheless, slow to find words on the spur of the moment, perhaps because few ever dared to taunt him. He admired Helgi for this gift, though he complained that he was lacking in spirit in other matters.

It was a mild autumn in the Tronderlaw, but about a week before the beginning of Advent there was a heavy fall of snow, and Helgi and Harald spent much of their free time, together with the other pages, on skis. The Norwegians were more skilled in this exercise than any Icelander, and among the housecarls of the royal garth there was a Finn from the north who would sometimes teach the boys new tricks. His most remarkable accomplishment was to shoot an arrow at a mark while traveling at high speed—he was a huntsman by trade. Sometimes Harald would persuade him to take them out after hares or ptarmigan on the fells; and they would set out on skis together, clad in skin jackets and hoods, each with his bow and quiver of arrows on his back, to spend the shortening hours of daylight gliding like the wind across the snow.

These were Helgi's happiest hours in all the time he was at court, and they were too few. For the most part he was irked and constrained by the lack of freedom. He liked the lessons well enough, in spite of the beatings they sometimes earned him, and the exercises in horsemanship and the use of arms were all right, too. But there was so much boredom and standing about—standing until his legs ached and he could scarcely keep his eyes open for weariness; there were too many long-drawn-out feasts and courts of justice at which he had to be present; too many audiences and deputations through which he had to wait attendance on the king.

He wondered sometimes at the king's patience and the seemingly tireless attention which he would give to even the most trivial matters; but it was no surprise to him that at the end of the day the king would often be short and irritable with those who were attending him. At these times it was usually one of the court scalds, either Sigvat or the young Icelander Thormod, who could do most to lighten his mood, and Helgi found some reward for the boredom of long feasts in the lays and ballads with which they were often followed.

One day Helgi was taking his turn in the great hall at

suppertime when he noticed a new guest whose dress and manner marked him out from the others at his table. He wore a knee-length tunic of scarlet silk, trimmed with white fur and a long cloak of the same material, lined entirely with fur and fastened at the shoulder with a gold brooch of unusual size. The hilts and scabbard of his sword were also heavily ornamented with gold, and on his wrist he carried a gerfalcon which he fed from his dish. He was no more than about twenty years old, but he seemed to treat the older men about him with something like disdain.

"What man is that?" Helgi asked one of the Norwegian pages. "He must be someone of importance, by the look of him."

He learned that the guest's name was Asbjorn, and that he came from Halogaland in the far north, where he had great riches and was related to the most powerful men in the land.

"He is a nephew of Thorir Hound, the king's landholder in the north," said the other boy, "and brother-in-law to Erling of Rogaland himself."

Asbjorn was a gay-spirited young man, open-handed and kindly toward those who treated him with a proper respect, as Helgi was soon to discover, but proud and inclined to truculence with any who tried to cross him. He seemed to be friendly with Thorarin, although they had little in common. The two would spend much time discussing the Finnish fur trade, in which Asbjorn's family had something like a monopoly, and Helgi deduced that his wily uncle was trying to win a concession from him. The king, however, treated Asbjorn with a marked coolness, and Helgi remembered the accusations

of heathen practice that were made against the Halogalanders.

Asbjorn and his followers left Nidaros as suddenly as
they had come, and Helgi learned from his uncle that
they had sailed their ship, a small merchant vessel, out
of the fjord by night, after an angry interview between
Asbjorn and the king.

"They wanted corn to take back to Halogaland, but
King Olaf forbade it," explained Thorarin. "I did my best
to speak for Asbjorn with the king, but to no purpose; he
said that there was not enough corn in Trondheim. Then
Asbjorn said that he would go south to his brother-in-
law, Erling, and buy corn of him, but the king told him
of the decree that he had made, forbidding the sale of
corn from one district to another, and said that such
supplies as there were in the south would be needed
when the court traveled southward in the spring."

"So Asbjorn has had to return home with nothing?"
said Helgi. His uncle shrugged his shoulders but would
not speak any more about it.

"Sigvat has told me that some of the Norwegian chieftains take it ill that they must obey a king," Helgi remarked to Harald the same day.

The younger boy replied, "When I am king, I will
make them obey, whether they take it well or ill."

Helgi said nothing to this, for he knew that there was
another heir to the crown of Norway before Harald; indeed, it was no secret at court that the king had had a
son by one of the serving-women there in Nidaros, and
the child was being brought up by the queen herself,
with her own daughter, Ulfhild. Once Helgi had overheard when Sigvat the Scald was telling the story of the

birth of Magnus, as the boy was named, and his own part in the naming of the king's son.

"Every man knows," he had said, "that when the king is asleep, then none must wake him, whatever the occasion, and that he who dares to disturb his sleep may do so at his own peril. Well, it so came about that the child was born at night, without the king's knowledge. And it was sick to the point of death, so that the priest came to baptize it and asked what name it was to be called. But the king was then sleeping, and I was there alone with a few of the women. So, rather than awaken the king and brave his wrath, I told the priest that the child was to be called Magnus, and it was so done. But when the king awoke the next morning and was told what had happened, he sent for me and asked how I had been so bold as to choose a name for his son without asking him. I replied that it was because I preferred to give two men to God, rather than one to the Devil. He asked what I meant by that, and I told him that the child was at the point of death, and if it had died heathen it would have belonged to the Devil, but now it would be God's, and I, too, I hoped, if the king decided to take my life for what I had done. Then the king was less angry, but he asked why I had chosen the name Magnus, when no one of his family had ever borne that name, and I replied that I had named the child after Charlemagne, the emperor, who had been the best man that I knew of in all the world. Then the king said, 'You are a lucky man, Sigvat. It is no wonder when good luck comes from wisdom; but when the deeds of a foolish man are turned to good fortune, that is a strange thing indeed.' And after that the child got stronger, and now he is sturdy and full of promise, and the king cherishes him above all things."

Helgi had seen little Magnus playing with his nurse—the mother had been sent away into the country soon after his birth—and he had wondered whether the luck of the great emperor, who had died more than two hundred years ago, would indeed follow him as King Olaf had foretold. Once he had spoken to Harald of his small nephew, but the other boy had shown little interest in the subject.

"Babies!" he had said scornfully. "They are a nuisance."

Seal-Thorir

The Yuletide celebrations at Nidaros were magnificent
and ceremonious, with three mitered bishops in the choir
of St. Clement's for the High Mass of the Nativity.

At the feast in the great hall, Queen Astrid was present
with her ladies in all their finery, and there was min-
strelsy and verse-making late into the night. Sigvat the

Scald received a gold arm ring from the queen, and he recited a poem in her honor.

After that, Thormod recited a whole series of verses that he had made for his lady, Kolbrun, in Iceland, and he was much applauded by all the womenfolk, who loved him for his dark eyes and wavy brown hair as much as for the subject of his verse. But the king said, "Give us a more manly lay, Thormod, such as will stir the blood of warriors that are become heavy with wine and ale." And Thormod replied with the ancient Lay of Bjarki that begins:

> Day is dawning,
> the cock claps its wings,
> time it is for thralls
> their tasks to tackle.
> Awake, now, awake,
> of friends the firmest
> and all the foremost
> of Adils' companions.

A short while after Yule, when the snow was frozen hard, Helgi and Harald were allowed to ride with the king to one of the royal manors, at Haug in Veradale, at the northern end of the Trondheimsfjord. While the king was attending to business with his steward in that place, a man named Thorald, and seeing those of his tenants who had any complaints or petitions to make, the two boys wandered off to explore the neighborhood. Not far up the valley they came to a poor-looking farm at the edge of a dense wood, and as they were crunching through the snow toward the house the sky suddenly began to get dark and a few large snowflakes floated down.

"Let's go back to the others," said Harald with a shudder. "I don't like this place."

Helgi, too, felt uneasy, as though unfriendly eyes were watching from among the dark trees, and it seemed to have become suddenly colder.

"Yes, we'll go back," he replied. "But let us first see what is beyond the top of the rise."

It was only a short way past the low huddle of farm buildings to the point where the track, rutted with sledge marks, disappeared over a hill. Above this the valley seemed to close in between wooded slopes and under a sky that had become blue-gray like hammered iron.

"There is somebody coming across the field behind the farm," said Harald as they trudged past the gable end of a barn with a broken roof. "He walks strangely, as though he were drunk. See how he feels with his hands along the turf wall."

"That man is not drunk—he is blind," said Helgi. He stopped walking and stared at the cloaked figure that was groping toward them.

"Why, what is the matter, Helgi? You have gone pale as skimmed milk," said Harald. When Helgi did not reply he continued, "I wonder what the old man is looking for. He is a beggar, by the sight of him. It would be a kindly deed to guide him past those outbuildings before he falls into the farmer's cesspool."

"Yes, of course." Helgi seemed to shake himself, as if trying to be rid of something. "It's foolish, but for a moment I took him for one who is now dead."

"He is no ghost," said Harald. "Look at the marks he

has made in the snow down by the wall. But what has become of him now? He went in behind the buildings, and now I see no sign of him."

"He'll be in one of the outbuildings, I dare say," said Helgi. "Let us be on our way, for I think there is going to be a heavy fall of snow. These are hard times for a poor man to be out in all weather," he added thoughtfully.

They walked on in silence up the track, which followed the curve of a stretch of open meadow above the farm. The snow was now beginning to fall thickly, and a light wind was blowing in chilly gusts down the valley, whirling the snowflakes in eddies into their faces. Helgi walked with bent head, leaning on the shaft of a hunting spear that he was carrying, deep in his own thoughts. Harald followed close behind, his cloak wrapped about him, his spirits oppressed by the eeriness of the place.

"Let's turn back to Haug," he said suddenly. "What's the sense in going further?"

Helgi stopped, but he did not answer. He seemed to be listening for something. Then Harald heard it too, a strange, haunted sound that sent a chill all over his body.

"Saints protect us, but what is it?" he asked.

"I don't know. It's something up the valley," said Helgi.

"That was no human cry. There it is again." Harald was pale now.

"Look!" Helgi clutched his arm and pointed through the eddying particles of snow. "Up on the hill there. A man watching us."

Harald's hand flew to the short *sax*, or dirk, that he carried at his belt.

"If it's thieves lying in wait for us, we'll show them something before we're done," he said. "But how still he stands up there. I'll fight any living man, Helgi, but with trolls and witches I'll have no dealings." He spoke boldly, but his teeth were chattering.

"There's something moving, away to the left there, on the hillside," said Helgi, and he lowered the point of his spear and strained his eyes to see through the snowflakes. He thought he could make out some gray shapes moving away toward the wood, but the figure above them did not stir. Then suddenly, leaning the butt of his spear on the ground, he began to laugh.

"That's no man, or troll, up there," he said. "It's just a stone standing in the middle of the meadow. And I know what is making that noise, too."

"What is it?" asked Harald.

"Wolves. Look, there they go up the valley. The sound of their howling must have been caught up and echoed between the hills to make that strange sound."

"I'm glad I was not here after dark to hear it," said Harald. "Wolves or none, it was a fearful sound."

"Now the snow has stopped and the sky is clearing," said Helgi. "Let us go as far as the stone and then turn back."

As they climbed the hill a ray of sunlight broke through the clouds behind them—an angry, red shaft sent out by the dying sun. It caught the stone above them, so that for a moment, in spite of its cape of drifted snow, it seemed to be bathed in blood.

Afterward, when they got back to Haug, they asked one of the housecarls the name of the farm up the valley.

He answered, "It is called Sticklestead—a poor place and of little note. It lies on the road that crosses the mountains into Sweden."

Easter was late that year, and the king decided to go south before the end of Lent and spend the holy season at one of his manors in Rogaland. Perhaps he was hoping to come to better terms with Erling, whom men called the "king of Rogaland."

It was arranged that the queen should travel overland, after Easter, direct to Tunsberg, where the king had a garth in his own country of Westfold near the mouth of the Oslofjord, and where he would join her in time for the great summer market in that town. After that they would probably spend some time at the royal manor at Sarpsborg, near the Swedish border. Harald, much to his annoyance, was to travel with the queen, while Helgi had managed to persuade his uncle Thorarin to let him sail with him on the *Heron,* which was bound with the king's fleet for the Tunsberg market.

It was a fine April morning with only a nip of frost in the air when the ships sailed out of the Trondheimsfjord. The long ships, picked from King Olaf's war fleet, went before, with the *Carlshead* in the lead. They were slender, shallow-draughted vessels of tremendous length, with only small sails, but with oars from stem to stern that sent them leaping at high speed through the waves. "Wave steeds," Sigvat the Scald called them, but to Helgi they looked more like sea serpents, with their curving figureheads and raised, tail-like sternposts. And, compared with the merchant ship *Heron,* broad in the beam and wallowing along heavily in their wake under its great sail, they were like grayhounds beside an old bull mastiff.

The *Carlshead*, with its painted head of a man, carved, they said, by the king himself—for he was a skilled wood carver—was covered from mast to steering deck by a striped tent that stretched on either side to the gunnels with their twin rows of painted shields. But Helgi was well enough contented with the rougher comforts and greater freedom of life on board the *Heron*, where he was out of reach of the anger of Bjorn the Marshal and the blows of the master of pages. When he heard that his uncle would be making the passage home to Iceland from Tunsberg that summer, he was filled with a sudden homesickness, but he dared not ask to return with him, lest he should be thought childish and unmanly. Nevertheless, he would gladly have faced any discomfort or misery at that moment for a sight of his own home and, to hide his feelings, he threw himself into the work on board ship with such a passion of energy that even Thorarin's sharp-tongued boatswain remarked upon it.

"We'd make a sailor out of him yet," he grunted.

The voyage from Trondheim southward along the coast in the bright spring sunshine helped Helgi to forget the hidden ache of homesickness, and soon he was giving himself up to the enjoyment of new sights as the majestic coast of Norway unfolded before them.

It was a leisurely journey, with frequent stops on the way while the king held *things*, or assemblies of the farmers, on islands or in fjords, or sat in judgment, or was entertained by his richer subjects. In almost every settlement, Helgi saw a church. Most of these were newly built, under the king's edict of Christian Law, either by the local people or their chieftain. Some had no priest but were served by a visiting Mass priest. Many of them, Helgi learned, were built on the sites of the old heathen temples, which had been meeting places of the districts for centuries past.

Helgi found little time to go ashore in these places, for, more often than not, the *Heron* caught up with the *Carlshead* and its escort just as they were about to weigh anchor; but in spite of this, the voyage south was so much delayed that the royal fleet had reached no farther than the district of Firths by Holy Saturday. The king therefore decided to attend the Mass of Easter at the chapel of St. Sunniva on the island of Selja, the place where he had landed on his return to Norway more than ten years before.

On the fifth day after Easter they arrived at the royal manor of Avaldsness, on the island of Karmt in Roga-land, and Helgi had to bid farewell to his short-lived freedom and return to his duties as a page once more.

The king's bailiff at Avaldsness was a man called Seal-Thorir. Helgi took an instant dislike to him. He was a man of humble birth who had been raised to a position of importance in the king's service, but he wore his authority badly, like the over-gorgeous dress that he assumed on the king's arrival. He strutted about among the pages with his silver-headed staff of office in his hand, ordering them hither and thither simply to show that he was a person of importance and equal to any chieftain's son, and he treated the thralls and housecarls with arrogance and contempt.

That evening the king was sitting at table and Helgi standing beside his elbow, when Seal-Thorir the Bailiff began to boast about the faithful manner in which he had carried out the royal commands.

"Between Michaelmas and the Feast of All Saints, lord," he said, "there came to me one from another district who offered much silver if I would disobey your edict and sell him corn. He was a man of noble birth and great wealth, and I am but the son of a thrall and of no account, except in your highness's favor. Nevertheless, I sent him empty-handed away."

"You did well, Seal-Thorir," said the king shortly. "What man was he?"

"Asbjorn of Halogaland," replied the bailiff, "a very proud young man, it seems, with his noble kinsfolk and his fine ways. But I humbled him in a way that he will not forget."

"So he did not accept the refusal that he had from me," said the king, frowning. "What then, Master Bailiff?"

"When I rejected his offer of silver, it seems that the young man went to his brother-in-law, who is no less a man than the great Erling himself." Seal-Thorir glanced about him nervously as he spoke. "Much is the ill will and many the slights that I have had to suffer from that man on your highness's behalf."

"Well," said the king impatiently, "even Erling would never dare break my express command, king of Rogaland though they call him."

"It is true, lord, for I have heard that when Asbjorn

bade his brother-in-law sell him corn, Erling replied, 'Little do you know of the king's might, up there in Halogaland, as we do here in Rogaland. But it may be that my thralls have corn to sell, for, as you know, the law is binding only upon free men.'"

The king's face went red when he heard this, but he said nothing, and Seal-Thorir continued, "Then Erling gave his thralls corn to sell to Asbjorn, and it was loaded on board his ship and he set off down the fjord until he reached this island of Karmt. But I had had wind of his dealings with Erling, so I boarded his ship with my men and forced him to put into land, and then I made him unload the corn to the last sack and carry it into the store here in Avaldsness."

"By the hammer of Thor, that was well done," exclaimed Bjorn the Marshal. "That will teach the Halogalanders to defy the king."

"Ah, but wait awhile, Master Bjorn," said the bailiff with a self-satisfied chuckle, "the story is not yet all told."

As he spoke, Helgi, who had moved forward to fill the king's cup, saw a dark figure move from the side door that led out to the kitchens, but he was too intent upon Seal-Thorir's story to give it much attention.

"I made Asbjorn help with his own men when we unloaded his ship," continued the bailiff. "I, the son of a thrall, gave orders to the pround chieftain, and he obeyed me."

"I think that must have been a bitter draught for him to drink," said Bjorn. "How did he take it?"

"Oh, well enough at first," replied Seal-Thorir with a grin. "But when I stripped the sail off his ship, it proved too much for him to bear. Then he broke down and wept in front of all."

The bailiff's high-pitched laugh stopped abruptly as a figure leaped out of the shadows, and there was a flash of steel in the firelight. Helgi saw Seal-Thorir slump forward at the king's feet, and at the same moment a heavy object fell with a thud on the table in front of the king. It was the bailiff's head.

Asbjorn of Halogaland stood before them with a bloody ax in his hands, but he let it fall to the ground and made no struggle when two of the guard ran up to seize him.

The king was pale with rage but he spoke quietly.

"Take him away," he said, "and let somebody clean up this mess," for the tablecloth before him was soaked in blood and his own garments were spattered with blood too. Helgi was sent out to fetch fresh clothes and, as he went, he saw Asbjorn being led away in chains by his guards. By the time he got back, most of the blood had been cleaned up and the bailiff's body taken away, but angry words were passing between the king and members of the court.

"Has the man been put to death, as I commanded?" King Olaf was asking, and one of the guard replied that he was being held in custody.

"Why has he not been killed at once?" asked the king.

Thorarin reminded him that it was considered an act of murder to kill a man at nighttime.

"Then he must die at sunrise," said the king. "He has earned death three times over: once for breaking the peace of Easter, once for killing a man in the king's chamber, and once for using my feet as a chopping-block. He shall die in the morning."

The following morning, the king rose early, according to his custom, and attended the morning office of Matins and Lauds in the church of Avaldsness. After that he held audience with some of the chiefs and notables of Rogaland, who had come to greet him, until it was time for Mass.

Helgi stood beside his uncle at Mass, and when they came out of the church the king walked over to Thorarin and asked him, "Is the sun high enough in the sky for us to hang your friend Asbjorn?"

There was a sneer in the way he said "your *friend*," but the Icelander looked him straight in the face for a moment before replying. Then he gave an awkward bow and said, "The bishop preached us a fine sermon last Friday, lord, at Hareid, near Selja. He told us that on that day the King of all power had suffered death, and that a man was more blessed who followed His example than the example of those who condemned and put Him to death. Today also is Friday, lord."

The king went red in the face and his eyes blazed, and for a moment Helgi shrank back, awaiting an explosion. But none came. Instead, the king seemed to gather himself, and with a smile he said to Thorarin, "So be it, I shall not have him put to death this day. But I shall hand him over to your charge, Thorarin, and your life will depend upon keeping him in safety until the time of his execution. See to it that he does not escape, my friend, for I should be sorry to lose you."

With that he turned on his heel and walked away.

Later in the day Helgi saw Asbjorn with Thorarin. He was pale and his clothes crumpled after the night in the jail pit, but he still carried himself haughtily for a man who had but a few hours left to live. Helgi wondered that his uncle had had the fetters struck off him and allowed him to walk about as he pleased in the king's garth.

"What if he tries to escape?" he asked when they were alone.

"Then my life would be forfeit for his," replied Thorarin with a smile. "But never fear, Helgi *minn*, he will not, for I have told him of the king's words, and he is an honorable man."

On Saturday morning there was a *thing*, or meeting, of the farmers of the district, and this dragged on well into the morning, so that Mass was later than usual and it was well past midday when the king sat down to dine. Besides this, he sat longer than was his wont drinking with his guests, for matters of importance had been brought to a satisfactory conclusion and he was in a good mood.

Now, according to the church laws established by the king himself, every Sunday and Holy Day had to be kept strictly from the time of the afternoon office of Nones on the previous day. Helgi knew this as well as any, but he did not understand why his uncle should be in such a hurry to attend the office, since he was lax enough in such matters in the normal way. Nevertheless, while the court was still at table, Thorarin called Helgi over and, in a whisper, bade him go to the priest of Avaldsness, who was sitting next to the bishop on the king's right, and ask him to ring the bell for Nones as soon as the king stood up from the table, whatever the hour might then be. Thorarin placed two large pieces of silver in Helgi's hand as a gift for the priest, telling him to be sure that his message was overheard by no man.

Somewhat puzzled, but anxious to please his uncle, Helgi took his chance while the bishop was deep in talk with the king. He leaned forward, as though filling the priest's goblet, and whispered the message. The priest did not say a word, but his eyes opened widely when he saw the silver in the boy's palm. He slipped his hand quickly over it, as if to restrain his pouring of the wine, and when Helgi lifted the ewer the silver was gone.

Not long after this, the king got to his feet and called out in a loud voice that some thralls should now be sent to take the murderer and put him to death. Several men went out, and Helgi saw the priest go with them. The king must have thought that he was going out to shrive the condemned man, for he nodded approvingly as he saw him go. But less than a minute later the bell of the church began to ring out with a rapid, high peal close beside the hall, and Thorarin stepped up to the king.

"Lord," he said, "whatever the man's crime, let him be spared on this Holy Day."

The king looked at him for a moment, and then he smiled.

"I do not know why you are doing this for him, Thorarin," he said, "and I think that you are playing tricks with me, which is a dangerous thing to do. But the man shall be spared until the Sunday is past. Watch him, though, for your own life depends on it. And on Monday he shall die, whatever you say or do."

On Sunday morning the bishop himself went to hear Asbjorn's confession and give him absolution, and at his request the condemned man was given leave to be present at High Mass, though under guard now, and in chains once more. He stood at the back of the church, near the door, with his guards.

Just after the reading of the Gospel was done, there was a commotion at the back of the church. Everyone except the king looked round to see what was happening, Helgi among them. He could see nothing, however, because of the great press of people in the church, and to make matters worse, some were pushing toward the door, while those outside seemed to be trying to get in.

The bishop was now intoning the Creed, but his voice was almost lost in the murmur of the congregation.

"What is it?" Helgi asked the man next to him. "What is happening?"

"Erling of Rogaland is come with a strong force of men and ships to rescue his brother-in-law," replied the man. "They say that a party of his men have just now entered the church and freed him. And here are we, caught like foxes in a trap, without a weapon to defend ourselves."

"But what about the guard?" asked Helgi. "Was there no warning?"

The man shrugged his shoulders. "Better ask *him* about that," he said, nodding toward the motionless figure of the king in front of them. "He will have every man at Mass."

Not until the Mass was ended did the king move. Then he bowed to the altar and walked slowly out of the church beside the bishop, people making way on either side and the court officials following behind, with Helgi among them.

When they reached the open doorway, the king

paused for an instant, and, looking past him, Helgi saw something that made his stomach go cold and his mouth dry.

The short distance between the church and the hall of the royal manor was lined on either side for every yard of the way with a solid rank of armed men, each man with his shield in front of him and his ax or spear held ready.

At the end, in front of the hall, stood a little group apart from the rest. One of them was Asbjorn and beside him stood a man taller by head and shoulders than any other there, with gray beard and hair under a cap of polished steel.

"Erling Skjalgsson," muttered a voice behind Helgi.

Very slowly, but without faltering, the king walked between the two ranks, the bishop and Bjorn the Marshal coming close behind him. Helgi followed, too, pressed from behind by others, though he tried not to look into the faces of the men behind the shields. The sun glanced in his eyes from helmet and ax and spear blade.

Then the king stopped, and the tall man stepped forward and greeted him with a bow.

"God be with you, Erling," said King Olaf. "What is your errand with me?"

"I have been told that my kinsman, Asbjorn, has behaved very ill, king," said Erling boldly. "It is bad that he has earned your displeasure. I have come to pay blood money for the fellow he killed and to buy his freedom."

"Erling," said the king, "it seems to me that you are taking it upon yourself to settle the matter for me, and that you have brought a force of armed men with you to back you up in your demands."

"You shall decide, lord," answered Erling, "whether or not there is to be a settlement between us."

"Are you trying to frighten me, Erling?" asked the king quietly. "I think that your force is not big enough for that. Have you forgotten that I did not flee before you at the battle we fought, when you were on the side of Earl Svein?"

Erling's face went as red as blood. "The odds were against me then, Olaf," he said. "You will find things different now."

Just then the bishop pushed forward past the king, his crosier in his hand, and spoke.

"Lord," he said, looking first at the king and then at Erling, "let there be peace between the two of you, for Norway's sake. Let Erling accept the king's doom on this man, provided that his life is spared, and exchange tokens for the holding of the truce."

"So be it," said the king after a long silence.

"I agree to that," said Erling.

There was an audible sigh of relief, and Asbjorn was brought forward to hear the king's doom. He held himself proudly while sentence was pronounced.

"There is a law," said the king, "that a man who slays the king's servant shall be himself bound to carry out his service, if the king wills it. It is my will now, Asbjorn, that you take over the office of Seal-Thorir, whom you killed, and become my bailiff here at the manor of Avaldsness."

"That is a generous doom," said the bishop.

"Let it be so," said Erling.

Asbjorn bowed slightly and then said, "I have but one

favor to ask. Will the king give me leave to go first to my own manor in the north and set things in order there?"

"You have my leave," replied the king, "but return before Whitsun."

Tunsberg

A few days later, Thorarin sailed in the *Heron* for Iceland, abandoning his idea of attending the market at Tunsberg. Helgi thought that it was because he was out of favor with the king, on account of his intervention for Asbjorn, but, before leaving, his uncle told him that he was to carry out an important mission at home.

"I shall attend the assembly of the All-*thing*," he said, "and talk with some of the leading men. I shall be back in Norway before the summer is out."

Helgi would have dearly loved to go with his uncle, but pride forbade him to ask, and besides, he knew that he would not be released from his duties.

The journey from Avaldsness to Tunsberg was uneventful, though to Helgi, now traveling on board the royal ship, the *Carlshead*, it was full of excitement. At first he expected to have a difficult time with the other pages, for there were some who were still frankly jealous of the favored position which he had won, and here he had to sleep and mess with his equals forward of the mast, while the king and all the chief men were in the after part of the ship, under the great striped awning that extended from mast to steering deck. Things might have gone hard for him, but for the intervention of his fellow countryman, Thormod the Scald. The young poet, though moody and temperamental, took a liking to him, perhaps because he was the only other Icelander on the king's ship at that time—Sigvat had stayed in Nidaros to go with the queen's party overland—and he soon made it clear to the Norwegian boys that Icelanders stand by one another.

They were less than a day out of harbor when Helgi fell foul of his old enemy Hauk. The younger boy had been sent forward to draw a pitcher of wine for the king from one of the large barrels that stood before the mast. On his way back to the stern he had passed close to Hauk, who had deliberately put out a long leg and tripped him, so that the wine had poured over the deck. For once Helgi had lost his temper. Forgetting time and place, he had flown at Hauk with all the fury of a small dog attacking a bull. He had thrown him on his back and was beating his head fiercely against the wooden planking when several other Norwegian pages decided to go to the aid of their comrade. Helgi found himself lifted like a sack of meal and hurled ungently down on the deck, and he was undoubtedly about to get the beating of his life when Thormod the Scald intervened, sending the other pages flying.

Fortunately for all concerned, the king's attention was elsewhere during this incident and Helgi escaped with a reprimand for his clumsiness in spilling the wine and was made to scrub the deck so that he would learn to be more careful. Hauk left him alone after this, but Helgi found excuse to spend as much time as possible aft in Thormod's company.

"Why is the ship named *Carlshead?*" he asked one day as he watched the crowned figurehead rise and fall as the bow breasted the ocean rollers.

"After the great emperor, Charles," replied Thormod. "The king admires him above all men, for he was the greatest Christian king that ever was."

"Of course," said Helgi. "That was why Sigvat named his son Magnus—after Charlemagne."

"The king carved the figurehead himself, you know," said Thormod. "He is skilled with his hands."

"King Olaf seems to do all things well," said Helgi. "Sigvat says that he is a good scald, too."

"You lay great store by what Sigvat says, boy," remarked Thormod, frowning. "It is true, though, that the king is a craftsman in words, as well as in wood and metal and, besides that, he is a skilled shot with the bow and a maker of good laws and a holy man at his prayers, like the bishop himself. I think that there is no other man like him, least of all a king, and he is one for whom a man might do worse than lay down his life."

"Why are you sometimes so sad, Thormod?" asked Helgi. "And why do you speak of dying?"

Thormod shrugged his shoulders but did not reply.

Later one of the guard told Helgi that Thormod's foster brother and dearest friend, who had himself been a guardsman and close companion of the king, had fallen at the hands of his enemies, and so Thormod had transferred all his love and loyalty to the king whom his friend had followed.

"You are a strange, deep lot, you Icelanders," the man said. "You are slow to move, but when you do move, then I think that I would sooner have you among my friends than my enemies."

Soon the fleet was skirting the gentler coastline and more fertile meadowlands of southern Norway as they turned northward into Vik, the great bay that lies between Norway and Sweden, and at last they came to Tunsberg, at the mouth of the Oslofjord.

Tunsberg was a larger town than Nidaros and much busier, for it was a meeting place for trade between all the nations about the shores of the Baltic and the North Sea. Helgi gaped in wide-eyed wonder when he saw the market square close to the harbor and the crowds of merchants gathered there with their wares.

There were Norwegians with the skins of bear, fox, marten, otter and beaver; Finns from the far north with reindeer antlers and magic charms; Swedes and Danes with slaves and ornamental silver and bronze work; Frisians with woven cloth; Saxons with Frankish swords and glassware from the Rhineland; Estonians with precious amber; and the men called *Russ,* in fur cloaks and baggy trousers, from the Swedish settlements south of Ladoga, with sables and squirrel furs and yet more slaves.

Beside these there were a few Icelanders with bales of woven cloth and stacks of dried fish, some Englishmen and Norse settlers from the west with silks and foreign wines to offer, and the crew of a ship from Greenland with walrus ivory and the priceless skins of white bears.

Here, for the first time in his life, Helgi heard the babel of strange tongues, and realized that the world was a bigger place even than all Iceland and Norway.

"Watch your purse in this crowd if you want to keep it," Thormod warned him as they threaded their way between the piles of merchandise and haggling traders. "There are as many thieves and rogues in Tunsberg as lice on a beggar's back."

The royal garth here was smaller than the winter residence in Nidaros and, indeed, was only used for short periods, since the king preferred his royal manor at Sarpsborg farther east when staying in the south of Norway. So long as the market lasted, life in Tunsberg was crowded and uncomfortable, but to Helgi at least it was not dull. However, young Harald, who had already spent some weeks there since his arrival with the queen and was heartily bored with his own company, was impatient for the time when the court would leave.

"We shall be free to do what we like in Sarpsborg," he said. "King Olaf spends most of the time attending *things* with the farmers, and the queen visits her brother across the border in Sweden. Here we must not move outside the garth without leave."

"Where is the guardhouse?" Helgi asked him.

"Where we shall not be going," replied Harald. "You and I are lodging with Master Geir the priest, Helgi, so that we can better attend to our studies. That's what the queen said. I shall be glad when we leave for Sarpsborg."

"Never fear," said Helgi, "we shall find things to do and to see while we are here."

And, in fact, there were matters both to see and talk about only a few days after Helgi arrived in the town.

The court had just returned from High Mass at the church of St. Michael when news was brought to the king that ambassadors of King Knut of Denmark and England were in the town and seeking an audience of him. The king's reply was clearly heard by all around him.

"Let them wait," he said. "King Knut will not be sending men to me but for his own gain." And he ordered the housecarls to set out the tables for dinner.

For three days the Danish envoys were kept waiting; but at last, word went round that the king had agreed to see them after supper that day, and a wave of excitement ran through the court as everyone waited expectantly to see what would come of the meeting. Sigvat, it was said, had spoken with the Danes and found them easy and courteous in their manner; but it was known that the Danish king had never given up the claim of his father, Svein Forkbeard, to the Norwegian crown, and that King Olaf had difficulty in keeping his temper if this subject was so much as spoken of in his presence.

"The king will send them home empty-handed, you will see," said Bjorn as they sat at table that evening. "He alone is the true heir of Harald Fairhair and rightful king of Norway."

"It will mean war with Denmark and England, then," said Calf Arnason, and others agreed with him.

"Let there be war, then," said Bjorn. "The chieftains and warriors of Norway are growing fat with too much good living."

"Let him speak who grows fat," said Thormod. "I for one am ready to eat or fight as the king wills."

There was laughter at this, and Bjorn went red in the face, for he was himself inclined to stoutness. But Sigvat, who was more silent and thoughtful than he had been at Nidaros, said that there were many among the Norwegian chieftains who looked with a favorable eye at King Knut, thinking that they had enjoyed more freedom in the days when Earl Hakon and Earl Eric had been viceroys of the king of Denmark, ruling over Norway, than they did now under the equal justice of King Olaf.

"He is a traitor that says so!" exclaimed Bjorn.

But Calf Arnason looked at Sigvat thoughtfully and said, "It is true that men of noble birth and ancient family are now made equal, under King Olaf's law, with baseborn men and peasants. It was for this reason that the thrall Seal-Thorir fell to the ax of Asbjorn, whom men now nickname Sealsbane. Every cockerel may strut and crow on his dunghill now, it seems."

"Seal-Thorir learned otherwise," said Thormod. "And I have heard that the Seal-Killer is likely to break his bargain with the king."

"Who has said that?" demanded Bjorn. "Asbjorn must

stoop his pride to the king's doom, for Erling himself has offered surety for it."

"It comes hard to you highborn Norwegians to stoop, even at the word of a king, it seems," said Sigvat.

Just then a horn sounded outside the hall.

"The Danes are come," said Thormod.

The king, seated in his throne at the other table, raised a hand for silence, and immediately the murmur of conversation died.

The Danish envoys, six in number, entered slowly by the great door with a tall gray-bearded man at their head. They were plainly dressed, with hauberks of Frankish ring mail under their cloaks and long swords hanging down. They advanced together until they were opposite the king and then bowed, and their leader stepped forward with a sealed letter which the king passed to Bishop Grimkel beside him. The leader of the Danes now spoke, and Helgi, standing close behind the king, could hear every word clearly, though he found the guttural Danish accent hard to follow at first.

"We bring you greetings, lord king, from our master, the most noble and Christian King Knut of England and Denmark. He bids us say that he wants peace with all lands, and for this reason he will not willingly come here with an army to take what is rightfully his, and so mar the peace of the land; but he reminds you, lord, that Norway is his by right, and by the right of his forebears, who governed it through earls before his day. Nevertheless, if King Olaf will go to our master and receive Norway of him as his fief, and become his man, and if he will pay the same taxes that the earls paid, then he may continue to rule over Norway in peace, and his descendants after him."

There was a complete silence and every eye in the hall was on the king when this speech was ended. King Olaf nodded, and then held out his gold cup to be filled. After he had sipped at the wine that Helgi poured with trembling hands, he turned to the bishop.

"Well?" he said.

"The words of the letter agree with what King Knut's envoy has just spoken, lord," said the bishop. "There are but some added details of the taxes paid by the earls Sigurd, Hakon and Eric. The letter is sealed in the king's hall of Westminster, on the feast of St. Augustine, in this year of Our Lord 1026."

The king stared into his cup and spoke without raising his eyes.

"In stories of old," he began, "I have heard it said that Gorm, king of the Danes, was considered a mighty king, although he ruled over Denmark only. But it seems that such is not enough for these Danish kings of more recent years. King Knut rules over Denmark and England, and he has won a large part of the land of Scotland besides; and yet he is now demanding my inheritance. Is there no limit to his greed? Does he intend to be king over all the northlands?"

King Olaf looked up suddenly and stared the Danish leader straight in the eyes with that terrible, cold, piercing gaze that those who knew him had learned to dread. The Dane went red and then pale and dropped his eyes.

"Tell your master this," the king continued. "Tell him that he alone will have to eat every cabbage in England before I will become his man—" there was a ripple of

laughter, but the flash of the king's eyes killed it almost
as it began. "Tell your master that I shall defend Norway,
which God has put into my hands, with all my strength
as long as I live, and that I shall pay no man tax for my
own domain."

The Danes left Tunsberg the next day, but not before
certain of the Norwegians had exchanged words with
them in private. So much Helgi learned from Thormod;
and he learned, too, that Sigvat the Scald had been
among their visitors, and even, it was said, Bjorn the
Marshal, himself. Helgi wondered whether the king
would have been angry to have heard about this, or if,
indeed, he knew—for some people said that he knew
everything. But one thing was certain, and that was that
the king was now in the best of tempers and nothing
seemed to disturb his good humor.

He spent much time meeting with the Upland farmers
at local *things*, or assemblies, and visiting churches with
Bishop Grimkel to see that they were being kept in proper
order and that the people were being taught the Christian Faith. On most of these journeys he would travel
with only one or two companions—Bjorn the Marshal,
Sigvat, the bishop and Master Geir the Chaplain, or
sometimes Thormod the Scald. Rarely were any of the
pages taken, and then usually the older ones, though
Harald sometimes went with the king to learn the duties
of kingcraft and the ancient customs of the *thing*.

"Magnus is my heir," the king would say, "but one day
you, too, Harald, will govern Norway." People wondered
at this saying, but Harald kept silent about it.

Helgi spent much of the time, when he was not with
Harald, in the bishop's garth, next to the church of St.

Michael where, with two young Norwegian clerks, he was learning Latin and the art of song from an elderly English priest. Such lore was not considered part of Harald's education, but Master Geir had recommended Helgi to the bishop as a likely pupil and a possible candidate for the priesthood. The king himself had warmly approved this addition to Helgi's studies, so that he was now released from many of his court duties and enjoyed a new freedom.

One fine summer day, however, the king was to attend a meeting of farmers only a few miles out of the town. Several of the pages were sick with a slight fever, and Harald was laid up on his bed with a swollen ankle after a fall from his horse, so Thormod the Scald obtained permission for Helgi to go with the king.

The day was so fine that, after the meeting, the king sent his escort on ahead with the horses, saying that he would walk back to Tunsberg through the meadows by himself. The page might come with him to carry his cloak, for it was very warm, but no guard was needed.

When Thormod protested and would have stayed behind, the king waved him on impatiently.

"Do you think that I am not safe here, in my own country of Westfold?" he demanded. "And if any were so bold as to lay a hand on me"—he slapped the hilt of his sword *Hneitir*, which means "Wounder" in the Norse tongue—"I am able to defend myself." Then he turned to Helgi and said, "You are the Icelandic priestling, aren't you? Well, come on. We have a good step to walk together."

Helgi had often been close to the king, and had sometimes been spoken to by him, but never until now had he enjoyed the rather alarming honor of being alone in his company.

At first he hung back at a respectful distance, walking in the king's footsteps, for the path was narrow, but taking care not to step on his shadow as it lay on the ground before him. They were following the line of a broad valley, with meadows to either hand and a little river, marked by a row of birch trees, winding along beside them away to the right.

After a while they came to a place where a wooden footbridge crossed the river, and their path was joined by another, widening to a dusty track.

The king now signed to Helgi to catch up with him and they walked side by side, though the boy kept his eyes on the ground ahead, not daring so much as to glance at the short, thickset figure beside him.

"How old are you, boy?" asked the king suddenly, making Helgi start and blush.

"Twelve . . . twelve years on this next feast of St. Anne, lord," he stammered.

"I hope that you pray often to the holy mother of Our Lady," said King Olaf. "She is a powerful protector of those that call upon her. So you are a whole year older than Harald? And yet I think that my young half brother is taller than you."

"The lord Harald is tall for his age, Highness," replied Helgi. "Everyone says so. He is very strong, too."

The king laughed. "Ay, he is big and strong, and will one day be a mighty warrior—mightier far than I," he said. Then his face clouded and he added in a low voice. "I think he will live to rule over Norway. But my mind tells me that he will die a violent death in a foreign land."

Helgi did not know what to answer, but he said, "Perhaps he will go to the Holy Land, lord."

The king smiled and replied, "You are a good boy. . . . What is your name, now?"

"Helgi, lord."

"Helgi . . . the Holy. Yes, I remember now. To be holy is all that matters in this world, Helgi. Remember that. I would have dearly liked to fight the heathen in the Holy Land, and maybe I shall yet, before I die. There is no death more blessed and holy than for a man to give his life for God and his faith. And yet a man must put his own house in order first."

"Yes, lord," said Helgi doubtfully, not knowing what he meant.

"Norway is my house, Helgi," continued the king. "I could not throw up my trust, that had been put into my hands by God Himself, even for the good of my own soul, now, could I?"

"Why, no, lord . . . I . . . I suppose not."

The king laughed. "No, Helgi, I could not. And keep this in mind, you, whose name means Holy—whether you become a priest or turn to sheep farming in that barren island of yours—that there are as many ways of being holy as there are men with tasks to perform."

"Lord," said Helgi, "forgive me, but there are some men coming along the road behind us."

"Then we shall have company on our way," replied the king. "Whatever happens, though, take care not to let them know who I am, no matter what they may say or do."

Helgi watched the newcomers anxiously as they came nearer. He alone was responsible for the king's safety, he told himself. What if the men were bandits or outlaws? He fingered the small knife at his belt, his only weapon, nervously. The men were making a great deal of noise for bandits. Clearly, they were not concerned about giving warning of their approach. More likely, they were a party of farmers returning home from some country fair, or from a wedding feast. They were talking and laughing loudly and from time to time they burst into song, and Helgi thought that their manner of walking betrayed the fact that they were the worse for drink.

When the men saw Helgi and the king, they hailed them energetically and speeded their pace to catch up with them. Then their leader, a big, black-bearded fellow who stood a good head and shoulders taller than the king, offered each a drink from a leathern bottle he was carrying.

"Well met, friends," he said in a thick voice. "Take a sup from this to speed you on your way."

The king sipped courteously at the bottle and, wiping it on his sleeve, handed it to Helgi, who did the same. The liquor was warm and harsh and very strong, and it made the boy cough and choke, to the amusement of the others.

"Whither are you bound, neighbors, on this bright and sunny day?" asked Blackbeard, taking a good pull at the bottle himself. "By your clothes, I'd say you must be townsfolk, the like of such as rob us honest farmers of the fruits of our toil with your hard bargains and high prices."

"It is true that we are from Tunsberg and are thither

bound, friend," replied the king, "but as for robbing honest farmers, that I declare that I have never done."

"Don't you believe it, Big Grim," said one of his companions, a small man with wispy, corn-colored hair. "He's a merchant, and most likely is come from buying some poor fellow's stock of corn for a quarter its value so that he can sell at four times the price in the Tunsberg market."

"If any merchant does such a thing, then he should be punished for it," said the king. "Surely, King Olaf's justice will protect all alike?"

"What does King Olaf know of it?" said Blackbeard scornfully, spitting in the dust. "Are you the one to tell him?"

The others laughed loudly at this and cried, "He's one of them himself. He's like the rest of them. Let's show him what we farmers of Westfold think of the townsfolk, Grim." And they began to get rough and boisterous with the king, jostling him and tripping his feet and kicking the dust of the road over his clothes.

"Stop, stop," cried Helgi, thrusting himself in front of the king. "You don't know what you are doing."

But the king gave him a warning glance, and a heavy push from Big Grim sent the boy flying. Then the farmers tumbled the king in the dust and rubbed his face in the road and threw dust over his hair, until at last they tired of their sport. After that, they went on their way, saying that they, too, were going to the town and would be glad to meet any merchant there who thought to overcharge them for their wares. "Tell your brother merchants that," shouted Big Grim. "Maybe we shall meet again."

"Maybe we shall," said the king, sitting up and wiping the dust from his eyes.

Helgi hurried to him, greatly upset by what had happened, and helped him to his feet, doing what he could to beat the dirt off his clothes.

"Lord," he said, the tears streaming down his face and making stripes on his cheeks, "pardon me, lord, but I could do nothing. They were so many . . ."

The king smiled rather ruefully and patted him on the shoulder.

"You were not to blame, Helgi," he said. "Do not worry yourself. Nevertheless," he added, "I intend to have speech with those farmers when we go to Tunsberg."

When they got back to Tunsberg the king said nothing of his dealings with the Westfold farmers. Nor did Helgi speak of it, knowing, without being told, that the king preferred him to be silent.

That same day, though, Helgi was sent with Thormod and another of the guard to find the men and bring them to the king. They were discovered without much difficulty in the market place. Helgi took care not to let himself be seen, while Thormod went up to Big Grim and bade him and his companions come to the royal garth, where King Olaf would have speech with them.

The farmers at once tidied themselves and combed their hair and beards, boasting to all around that they were called for by the king, and then strutted off behind Thormod. Helgi slipped on ahead and took up his place in the hall behind the king's throne, and it was not long before the guard at the door announced the arrival of those for whom the king had sent.

The men advanced unsuspectingly to the place where the king was sitting, bowed, and then stood with a horror of dawning recognition breaking out in their faces.

"So, friends, we meet again," said the king in a quiet voice which those who knew him had learned sometimes to dread. "I think that at least I owe you a cup of wine for our meeting on the road."

Big Grim threw himself on his knees before the king, and his companions did the same.

"Pardon, lord . . . we did not know . . . forgive us. If we had known—"

"What have these men done?" asked Bjorn the Marshal curiously, but the king did not answer him. He was looking at the farmers, whose teeth were chattering with fear as they knelt before him. What would the king do with them? Helgi wondered. Would they be put to death at once? Or would they be imprisoned, or maimed, or perhaps banished for life? He felt pity for them, because they had offended in ignorance; but the enormity of their crime in the king's eyes—that of raising their hands against his sacred person—precluded any lesser doom.

"Boy, fill cups for these good men," commanded the king. "They must be allowed to drink my health, now that they know who I am."

"Lord, if we are to die, then let it be at once," said Big Grim. "Do not make sport with us." But the little farmer with corn-colored hair pleaded with raised hands that their lives should be spared.

"My friends, I mean to do you no harm," said the king. "What you did against me, you did unknowing. But I would have you remember to treat wayfarers more gently in the future. Like the disciples of Our Lord at

Emmaus, you know not at any time with what manner of man you are walking; and you should learn to see Christ, too, in the stranger on the road."

Then the king made the farmers sit down with him and drink, and when they left the royal garth they swore that King Olaf was a man after their own hearts and they would serve him to the death.

"It is not difficult to win the friendship of the poor and humble," said the king after they had gone. "It is the rich and powerful that are sparing with their love."

Helgi wondered what he could mean by this, for surely if any man was blessed with true and faithful friends, it was King Olaf. But more than this he wondered at the gentle and forgiving spirit of the king, who could, he knew, be so hard and ruthless to his enemies.

"King Olaf is a true follower of the Master whom we all serve," said Geir the priest, when Helgi spoke to him of what had happened. Harald had been scornful, saying that his brother prized his kingship too lightly, that the men should not have been allowed to go unpunished, but Geir would have none of this.

"No man sets a higher price on the sacred dignity of kingship," said the priest; "but King Olaf will win men by gentleness when he can. Only against the power of the Devil he will use every strength that he has."

"Master Geir, tell us the story of Gudbrand of the Dales," pleaded Helgi. "I have heard others speak of it, and now Harald says that they rode through Gudbrandsdale on their way here from Trondheim."

"Yes," said Harald, "and I saw Gudbrand in the new church there. He's a big, red-bearded man, ugly as a troll. I wonder that my brother ever made a Christian out of *him*."

"But five years past, a heathen temple stood on the very spot where that church is today," said Geir. "I was with the king when he went there—also old Bishop Sigurd, who was bishop in King Olaf Tryggvason's day. But this is no time for stories. . . ."

"Tell us, Master Geir," begged Helgi. "We will make up for the time later."

"Well, since it is part of the history of our holy Faith here in Norway . . ." said the priest; and he told them the story of King Olaf and Gudbrand of the Dales.

"Even at that time, many of the inland parts of Norway were beyond the king's edict and still in the darkness of heathen ways, with their secret, devilish superstitions of blood and wickedness and forbidden rites. So it was in the great inland valley of Gudbrandsdale a bare five years past, until King Olaf came there with a force of arms and the Bishop Sigurd, preaching the Christian Faith.

"Gudbrand of the Dales was a mighty chieftain in those parts, almost as powerful in his own country as Erling of Rogaland in his. He was a worshiper of the god Thor, of whom he had a great idol in the temple on his estate. When he heard that King Olaf was on his way with the new Faith, he sent out the war arrow to all his people and gathered an army to oppose the king, and the great image of Thor was carried out of the temple and set up in the place of assembly. It was made in the shape of a man with a hammer in his hand, covered with gold and silver and precious ornaments, and was hollow inside.

"Gudbrand now sent part of his force against the king, under the command of his son, a youth of eighteen years; but things went against them and the boy was made prisoner. Then King Olaf sent a message to Gudbrand, telling him that he wished to hold a *thing* with all the farmers of the valley, and he offered a truce for as long as the *thing* continued. This was agreed, for Gudbrand thought that the sight of Thor would strike terror into the hearts of the Christians.

"That night the king sent men secretly to drive away all the horses on which the farmers had come there and to bore holes in the boats in which some of them had rowed up the river. Then he called to him a man named Kolbein the Strong, who was always armed with a great club, and bade him stand close beside him the next day. After that the king spent all the night in prayer in his tent, until it was time for Mass.

"The next morning at the place of assembly Bishop Sigurd stood up in cope and miter and with his staff in his hand, and preached the gospel of Christ before all the people. The farmers listened quietly, but one of Gudbrand's followers, a chieftain named Thord Paunchbelly, said, 'He has a deal to say, this horned one who holds in his hand a stick with a crooked ram's horn on top, but he has not shown that his god is more powerful than ours.'

"Then Gudbrand ordered the image of Thor to be carried into the middle of the assembly, and he called out, 'Now where is your god, King? I think he must be holding his head low, like you and the horned one that sits beside you, now that our god is here in all his might. Do you dare to look Thor in the eyes, King?'

"The king whispered a few words to Kolbein the Strong, who was standing, club in hand, at his side, and then stood up and said in a loud voice, 'Look to the east, where our God comes in glory of light!'

"All the assembly looked to the east, and the eyes of every man were dazzled by the rising sun, and at that moment King Olaf gave a nod to Kolbein, who at once ran forward and struck the idol a mighty blow with his club.

"It broke in pieces, and out of it ran mice as big as cats, and lizards and snakes, and all the heathens turned in terror and ran for their horses and boats, but found that they could not get away, for the king's men were on every side of them with weapons ready.

"Then King Olaf summoned the *thing* once more and spoke to the people, and he said, 'I cannot understand why you run away in such fear. You can now see for yourselves the power of this god of yours, and what creatures have had the benefit of the food and other offerings that you have put before it. People who persist in such foolishness are sure to suffer for it, so now I advise you to pick up all the gold and silver and ornaments that are lying scattered on the ground there, and give them to your womenfolk. If you want to fight with us, we are ready, and the God in whom we believe will give the victory to the one he chooses.'

"Then Gudbrand stood up and said, 'Our god has been of little help to us. We will accept the God whom you worship, King.'

"After that the bishop baptized Gudbrand and his son,

and priests were left there to teach the people, and a little later Gudbrand himself built the church that stands at this time in Gudbrandsdale.

"From this story," said Geir the Priest, "you may see for yourselves that King Olaf is ready to deal gently with men if they will listen to reason, in spite of the hard things that some of the chieftains say against him."

"Bjorn the Marshal says that the edge of an ax is the only reason to which the chieftains will listen," said Harald; but Helgi was thinking that Thormod the Scald had been right when he said that for such a king a man might do worse than lay down his life.

Travels and Grave Tidings

The summer market at Tunsberg ended on the feast of
Saints Peter and Paul, and the stalls and traders' booths
were taken down and the market square stood empty.
The court was due to leave the next day for the manor
of Sarpsborg, on the Swedish border.

That evening a ship arrived at the town jetty. It was

the *Heron* and on board were Thorarin Nefjolfsson and
a party of men from Iceland. Helgi was surprised to hear
of his uncle's arrival, not expecting him back from Iceland so soon, though he knew that he had sailed on the
king's business.

"The belated guest finds the table empty," remarked
Sigvat when he was told of it; but he and Thormod both
went down to the jetty to meet the Icelanders and hear
the latest news from home. Helgi would have gone too,
but he was kept busy with a task for Master Geir until
the bell rang for Vespers.

When the king came out of church, Helgi saw his
uncle with Sigvat and Thormod and a group of young
men coming toward the hall. Thorarin greeted King Olaf
and spoke with him for a while. Then the young men
came forward in turn and saluted the king, and by their
names Helgi knew that they were sons of some of the
leading men in Iceland: Egil Hallsson, Thorodd Snorr-
ason, Gellir Thorkelsson, Stein Skaptason. Why were
they here in Norway so late in the summer, he wondered.
Afterwards he learned that his uncle had taken a bell to
Iceland as a gift from King Olaf for the church at Thingvale, the Icelandic place of Assembly, with a request that
the country should be brought under Norwegian law in
return for the king's friendship and protection. The Icelanders had taken the offer rather coldly, he was told.
Thorarin had returned with a vague reply, but since his
countrymen wished to stay on good terms with their
Norwegian kinsfolk for reasons of trade, the leading men
among them had sent their sons to Norway as a token
of their good will.

"It is in my mind," remarked Sigvat, "that King Olaf

will have his hands full dealing with the bears and wolves in his own land, without hunting the foxes on that island of ours."

It turned out that Thorarin had news to tell of at least one of the Norwegian wolves, as it happened. On the voyage to the south he had put in at Avaldsness, on the island of Karmt. Here he had learned that Asbjorn Sealsbane, the slayer of the king's bailiff, had broken his word to the king, not having returned from Halogaland, where he was said to be in deep conspiracy with his powerful kinsmen Thorir Hound and Erling.

This news cast a gloom over the court, but it was eclipsed in Helgi's mind by tidings of a more personal kind, which brought his whole world tumbling about his ears.

He learned about it after supper that evening, when the king sent for him to come at once to his sleeping chamber. Thorarin was there with the king, his long, ugly face looking unusually solemn.

"Boy," said King Olaf, "how do you like to be here with me?"

"I like it well, lord," replied Helgi, wondering at the question.

"It seems, nevertheless, that we must lose you," said the king. "Your first duty lies with your own family."

"There is bad news from home, Helgi," said his uncle. "Your father fell from his horse on the way to the *thing*. He has not got up from his bed since, and the leeches have little hope of his recovery. Your mother is in sore need of help on the farm, for your brothers and sisters are too young to do much. With King Olaf's leave, you are to return home with me this autumn."

Helgi's heart leaped at the words, but at once he felt ashamed to be glad when his father was sick—perhaps dying—and he was leaving the king whom he had learned to love. He longed to see his own country again, with the deep, fierce longing of an exile—the longing which, by a sudden insight, he understood to be behind the moody changes of Sigvat and the gloom of Thormod—but he had begun a new life, with new loyalties and new hopes, and it was a cruel thing to be tearing himself away when these new roots had just begun to take hold. To serve God and the king in the Holy Order of priesthood—

"You must go, Helgi," said the king gently. "Your mother and your brothers and sisters need you."

When Helgi took leave of his comrades and those whom he had come to regard as friends, he felt ashamed and guilty, although he knew that the king was right and he must go.

"I'm sorry for you, going back to that place," said Harald, "especially now that we are sure to be having a war with the Danes."

Geir the Priest bade him hold fast to all that he had learned and not forget the calling for which he had been singled out by God's providence and the king's favor.

"You must come back to Norway as soon as you can, boy," he said, "but in the meanwhile I shall give you a letter to any bishop or godly person that may have authority in your land. . . ."

Sigvat said, "Go in luck, Helgi. You have known a great king and a man worth serving. It may be that things will be different here in the future."

"I shall come back," said Helgi, but Sigvat shrugged his shoulders.

"No man knows what Fate has in store for him," he said. "Go to Iceland and live your life with a quiet mind."

The next day the king sailed for Sarpsborg, and Helgi was left behind to help his uncle get the *Heron* ready for the voyage home. One of the other Icelanders, Gellir Thorkelsson, was returning with them as the king's emissary, with a letter for the Icelandic Assembly.

Two days later the *Heron* put out to sea with a stiff southeasterly wind. By midday on the following day, the coast of southwest Norway had dropped below the horizon on their starboard quarter and they were setting a course for home.

Iceland is a rocky, wind-swept land of towering glaciers and snow-capped mountains, of barren moors and rugged lava fields, of wide plains and mighty rivers; a land where man and beast shelter indoors all through the long, dark winter, while the snow lies deep outside, but where the summer brings out a multitude of wild flowers, and the green, fertile valleys are warm in the sun.

Here Helgi returned to the life that he had always known, except that now it brought him new responsibilities at an age when most boys were still obeying their elders. Now it was he, under his father's guidance, who gave the orders and saw to it that they were carried out by the housecarls and thralls. It was he who rode out with the shepherd after lost sheep on the fells, who lay in wait with his father's bow for the fox that was preying on the newborn lambs, and who watched the weather with an anxious eye while the homefolk harvested every blade of grass in the meadows for winter hay.

Sometimes, when he was alone with his thoughts on the fells, he would remember the times—now so distant—when he had longed for his own company; when he had been wearied by the bustle of court life and the irritating chatter of Harald, ever beside him. To be alone, he had thought then, just for a little while, so that he could have time to think about some of the things he had seen and heard; so that he could possess his soul in peace—that was what he had longed for.

But now that he had his wish, he felt a strange emptiness, as if the tide of life had cast him up on a deserted shore and left him high and dry. Something was happening out there, in the great world beyond the rim of the sea, but he had no part in it.

He was fond of his family, but somehow he seemed to have grown away from them all: his brothers and sisters, with their practical jokes and childish laughter; his mother and father, with their anxious care about trivial things and their interests bounded by the narrow confines of the district.

His father had taken a turn for the better the summer after Helgi's return, but it was clear that he would never be a whole man again, and the most he could do was hobble about the farm with a stick and see that the buildings were kept in a good state of repair and the turf roofing renewed when necessary.

A second winter came, and most of the time Helgi's thoughts were too much occupied with the day-to-day problems of the farm to find a place for what might be happening across the sea in far-off Norway.

Occasionally, though, a faint echo of news from the greater world would reach them in Islefirth, and in the long winter evenings—while the homefolk sat round in the *stofa* and combed wool or knitted, listening to an old ballad, or to sagas of giants and trolls, of ancient gods and heroes and of kings and earls in other lands—Helgi's mind would sometimes turn rather sadly to the days that already seemed so long ago, when he had lived in a palace and served a king.

"It is not like that," he would say. But when they asked him what he meant, he would shrug his shoulders and reply that it was no matter, and his mother would look at him with a worried frown and shake her head.

Once a traveling peddler came to the farm and told of the alliance that King Olaf of Norway had made with his brother-in-law, the king of Sweden, and how together they had harried the coasts of Denmark and carried off much booty, and Helgi felt a pang of envy to think that Harald had probably sailed on that raid and how he would boast of his deeds against the Danes.

The following spring, though, the news was bad. It seemed that many of the Norwegian chieftains had wearied of King Olaf's rule and had accepted gifts of King Knut. Among these men were Erling of Rogaland and Thorir Hound, to whom it was said that Knut had promised an earldom.

That summer Helgi took time off from the farm to ride to the Assembly at Thingvale with his chieftain, Eyjolf of Maddervale. He was a son of Gudmund the Mighty, who had died while Helgi was in Norway. For the occasion, Helgi put on his best dyed clothes that he had laid aside since his homecoming—he had almost grown

out of them, but his mother altered them to fit him—and
as he rode across the high moors with Eyjolf and his
thing-men, he felt almost as if he were riding behind King
Olaf once more to a farmers' *thing* in Upland or the
Tronderlaw. Maybe he would have news of his old master
at Thingvale, he thought, for the yearly meeting of the
Assembly was a great occasion for the exchange of news
from all parts of the country and from lands beyond the
seas.

To his surprise and pleasure, after they had got to
Thingvale and stabled their horses in among the booths
set aside for the men of the Northern Quarter, almost the
first person Helgi walked into beneath the Law-Rock was
his uncle Thorarin, lean and ugly as ever, but looking
older and grayer than when he had last seen him.

"Come in luck, kinsman," said Thorarin rather gloomily.
"You are grown to be a man since we met. What are the
tidings from Islefirth?"

"Good," replied Helgi. "My father has mended, and
can walk about, but he can do no heavy work. All is well
with us on the farm. But what is your news, Uncle? Are
you come from Norway? How does King Olaf fare, and
what truth is there in the rumors that are told here of
treachery and broken promises?"

"I put out from Tunsberg fourteen days past," replied
Thorarin, "and struck foul weather off the Shetlands,
with the loss of three men and much of my cargo. The
news from Norway is bad for those that love King Olaf.
This spring the Danes gathered a great fleet, and a sea
battle was fought off the Holy River, in which neither
side had the advantage. But since then the Swedes have
thought better of their alliance with Norway, because

of the might of King Knut, and many of the leading
Norwegians have turned against King Olaf, too."

"Erling of Rogaland?" said Helgi.

"Erling fought against the king at the Holy River, but
he is now dead," said Thorarin. "The king pursued and
caught him and overpowered his men."

"And Erling died fighting. . . ." said Helgi, thinking
of the proud old chieftain who had defied the king at
Avaldsness. "He would be welcomed home by the warriors of heathen Valhall, the Hall of the Slain, if such were
not a lying tale," he said sadly.

"It was not so," said Thorarin in a low voice. "I was
with the king when it happened. Erling was taken alive
and brought before him, and the king—"

"The king did not have him put to death for revenge,"
exclaimed Helgi. "That he would never do."

"The king was holding his great ax when Erling was
led to him," replied Thorarin. "His eyes flashed when he
saw the man who had hindered him so much, there in
bonds, bareheaded and helpless before him. I think that
he could not contain himself for triumph, that one so
great had been brought low, for he raised his ax and,
with the horn of it, cut Erling on the cheek, and as he
did so, he said, 'The traitor must be marked.'

"Whereupon one of the king's men, Aslak Askelsson,
who was Erling's enemy, ran forward and struck Erling
on the head with his sword, so that he fell dead. Then
the king said to Aslak, 'May you be accursed for that
blow. Now you have striken Norway out of my hands!'"

Helgi was silent for a moment. Then he said, "That was
an unlucky blow, indeed, but I think that with it Aslak
has rid King Olaf of a dangerous enemy."

"He has also lost him many friends among the Norwegians," said Thorarin. "Calf Arnason, of the guard, has joined Knut, and even Bjorn the Marshal has gone back to his estate. King Olaf left his ships in the Oslofjord and has gone north overland to try and win support from the people of Trondheim. If he fails, it is said that he may have to cross into Sweden and take refuge with his brother-in-law."

"I think that King Olaf will never give up Norway, so long as he has a man left who will follow him," said Helgi. "That Calf and Bjorn should have deserted him, though!" His mind seemed stunned by the news, so that he could not think for a while. Then he was filled with a great longing to be with his old master again, and he said, "Uncle, why are you not with the king now, you that were his friend from the earliest days?"

Thorarin avoided his eyes as he replied. "I am getting old, Helgi," he said. "And besides, what have I to do with the Norwegians, whether or no they have a king, and if he be a Norwegian or a Dane? If his own people do not want King Olaf, what is it to me? I have been somewhat out of favor with him since the matter of Asbjorn Sealsbane, after my mission here to Iceland came to nothing."

Helgi turned away and said in a low voice, "I had no right to ask you this, kinsman. I should have been asking myself the same question. He trusted me and let me go when my need was great."

"King Olaf has many to serve him," said Thorarin gently.

"Not so many now, by your telling, and I think his need cries out for every man that owes him service. Not you, Uncle," Helgi added quickly. "You have paid your debt, and more."

"But your father, boy, and your family," said Thorarin.

"My father has help now and can manage without me," Helgi answered. "Should I lurk here, like a fox in a hole?" he continued. "I must go back to the king. I must go back before it is too late."

Thorarin looked at him and shrugged his shoulders.

"Some would say that a foolish man leaves his own hearth in a storm, unbidden, to look for another's lambs," he said. "But I think that you will go if you have made up your mind to."

Helgi bought himself a passage on a Norwegian merchant vessel there at the *thing,* and was on the sea within two days of the breaking up of the Assembly. His uncle had lent him money and an outfit for the voyage, and had promised to explain his decision to the people in Islefirth.

"A man must keep faith if he is to hold up his head among his friends," Helgi had said. Thorarin had said nothing in reply, but had pressed his hand on parting and bidden him bear greetings to King Olaf and tell him that he had not forgotten their former friendship.

Helgi chafed at the delays and contrary winds that held up their passage to Norway. By the time they at last anchored off Tunsberg, the year was already far advanced. Reports in the town were vague and conflicting. Some said that King Olaf had fought a great battle in the north and driven his enemies into the sea; others said that King Knut's men were in control of all Norway west of Lindesness. Earl Hakon Ericsson was back in

Trondheim—he that had once sworn never to fight against King Olaf—and was ruling as Knut's viceroy. The king had been wrong to spare his life, men said, for he had great support among the farmers of the Tronderlaw. As for Calf Arnason and Bjorn and others who had left the king, it was said that Knut the Dane had offered rich gifts to those that would change sides, and Sigvat the Scald had made a bitter verse about them. And yet there were some men who said that even Sigvat himself had received gifts of the Danish king.

"That I will not believe," said Helgi, but he felt uncertain and miserable, not knowing whom he might trust or who was telling him the truth. He decided to cross over the mountains to Trondheim as soon as he could get horses for the journey, but here he ran into difficulties. Nearly every available horse had been commandeered by the king on his march north, and those that remained were not to be bought for money. Helgi made up his mind to attempt the long journey on foot, and he set off as the first snows of winter were beginning to fall.

The overland journey took him no more than three days' walking north of Tunsberg, into the district of Ringeriki, where disaster befell him.

He was making his way alone through the edge of a great pine forest on the shores of a lake. It was a clear, still day and the woods were very silent, but for the occasional scurry of a bird in the undergrowth or the muffled thud of snow falling from a tree.

He walked fast, stepping where he could in the broad ruts made by sled runners along the road, but his thoughts were with the king, wondering how he had fared in the north against Earl Hakon, and whether he was back in the royal garth at Nidaros.

The ambush caught Helgi completely by surprise. All he heard was a creak in the snow behind him, and then a coarse material was flung over his head and his arms pinned to his sides. He struggled wildly but could not free himself, and the next moment he was on his face with someone heavy pinning him to the ground.

"'Tis naught but a boy," he heard a rough voice saying. "Let's take a look at him." Then the cloth was pulled off his head and he was allowed to sit up.

He saw three ruffianly figures in leathern jerkins and hoods staring down at him. They were all armed with bows and axes and their leader made no doubt as to their intentions.

"Take the purse from his belt," he said, "and let me see what's in it."

"You'll pay for this," exclaimed Helgi.

"Not so," said the robber. "You are the one who will pay, and not so ill either, it seems. You are a foolish young man to be walking the roads alone in these times."

"There was a time when the king's law was a hand of protection over every traveler," said Helgi bitterly. "There was sharp justice then for such thieves as you."

"When big thieves rule, then small thieves have their day," replied the robber with a wink at his companions. "Because you are young, boy, we'll let you go on your way, in spite of your bold speaking. But your silver will stay with us."

"Never fear but King Olaf will catch you and hang you on the tallest tree in the forest for this," fumed Helgi. "The king is my friend and will avenge my loss."

"Young master, you will live longer if you keep your tongue better than you have kept your money," said the robber with a grin. "King Olaf's friends are the ones who dance from the tallest trees, these days. But because the king was a good man and loved the poor, I will give you some advice. More than that, I will give you some of your money back—though we can ill afford it and it goes against our trade—because I and my comrades are true Norwegians. Do not go north, for King Olaf is no longer in Norway."

"I'll never believe that," cried Helgi. "He would not give up his kingdom."

"Nevertheless, it is true," replied the robber, and he spat as he added, "Most of his rich and powerful friends deserted him when they heard that Earl Hakon was come into Trondheim with a great army and many ships. I have heard tell that the king made his way with a few of his folk across the mountains into Sweden."

"He will come back," said Helgi. "I know that he will come back when the time is ripe."

"That may be so," replied the friendly robber, "but you take my advice, young master, and turn back before you run into Earl Hakon or any other of King Knut's men, who are giving short shrift to all that will not swear for the Danes."

"Where can I go if all Norway is in their hands?" asked Helgi despondently. "I shall have to follow the king into Sweden. There is nothing else for it."

"Why not join with us?" said the robber. "There are many true Norwegians taken to the forest in these times."

Helgi shook his head. "No, I must go to the king. I shall turn eastward through Vingulmark and cross to the other side of the Oslofjord. Maybe I can reach Sweden before the winter snows fall."

"You'd be wiser to wait for the spring, boy," said the robber. "I have heard that there are many still faithful to King Olaf on this side of the border, round Sarpsborg. Most likely they will have news of the king there, and what he intends to do. Here, take this"—impulsively he thrust into Helgi's hands the leathern pouch in which he had carried his money—"they always told me my heart was bigger than my head," and he turned to his two companions, as though daring them to challenge what he had done.

"Come, lads," he said, "let us go and rob some Danes."

Helgi was four days reaching Sarpsborg, and on the last day there was a fall of snow so heavy that it was all he could do to reach the royal manor before nightfall. Here he would rest a day or two, he thought, and find out what he could about the king. And he would buy himself skin clothes and a pair of skis for the journey into Sweden.

On the way he had taken care to learn what he could about the folk at Sarpsborg. At least the place had not fallen into Danish hands, for Knut's men had kept away from the east side of the Oslofjord for fear of trouble with the Swedish king. Harald Sigurdsson, the king's young half brother, was there, and Bishop Grimkel, and several other leading Norwegians. How surprised they would be to see him, Helgi thought.

He was not prepared, though, for the warmth of his reception at the gate of the garth. The sentry took him for a spy and at once had him thrown into the jailhouse, and it was only after a cold and uncomfortable night there that he was recognized by another of the guard, Thord Folason by name, and set free. He went at once to the hall and asked for Harald.

At first he did not know the tall, richly dressed boy who rose to greet him.

"Helgi the Icelander, by the Holy Saints!" said Harald. "I little expected to see you here. Welcome a thousand times."

"Where is the king?" asked Helgi. "I have heard bad news of him."

"It could not be much worse than the truth," said Harald. "He has gone to Sweden to get help from his brother-in-law, King Onund-Jacob, but I fear that his errand will bear no fruit, for the Swedish king has made peace with the Danes."

"And what are you doing here in Sarpsborg?"

"Waiting for better times," replied Harald. "There are many true Norwegians here who would be glad to rid themselves of the Danish domination over Norway, if the time were ripe." And he told Helgi how the land had slipped back into lawlessness and violence in the past year, and how the chieftains had each become king in his own district, as in the old heathen times, and every man's hand was against his neighbor. His eyes flashed as he said, "If I were but a few years older I would win back the kingdom of my brother, but these old men speak only of peace."

"Knut is a Christian king and has sworn to safeguard the rights of the Church," said Bishop Grimkel. "He will establish order in time. In the meanwhile we must pray that God will give back to Norway its true king."

"Prayers," said Harald, "will avail little against Danish axes."

"Where is the queen?" asked Helgi, and he was told that she had gone into Sweden with King Olaf to beg help of her brother. Thormod the Scald was with them, too, but Sigvat had gone abroad.

"He was friendly with Knut, it seems," said Harald bitterly, "in spite of the verses he made against traitors."

"You should not judge him, my son," said the bishop. "I have heard that he meant to go on a pilgrimage to Rome for his soul's sake. God alone can read the hearts of men."

"I shall follow the king into Sweden," said Helgi. "I see no sense in waiting here."

Harald shrugged his shoulders. "I would have done the same long since," he said, "but all say that he will return to Sarpsborg in the spring and that it is better to wait for him."

"You will serve the king best by waiting," said the bishop. "What can you do alone? This winter I shall go back to Tunsberg to care for the souls of my flock. But it may be that in the spring there will be tidings from Sweden."

It was a cold, hard winter in Sarpsborg, with little to relieve the gloom of the long, dark evenings but the memories and hopes of angry and disappointed men.

About Yuletide they heard that King Olaf had left Sweden empty-handed and had crossed the Eastern Sea into Holmgarth, the lands of the Swedish colonists known as the *Russ*. Here he was living with his son, Magnus, and a few followers at the court of the Russian king, Yaroslav, to whom he was connected by marriage, and it was said that he was held in high honor by the people there.

"He will never come back now," groaned Helgi when he heard this news, and Harald agreed that it seemed unlikely.

"You are the last of the line of Harald Fairhair," Helgi said. "What will you do?"

Harald shrugged his shoulders. "The people of Norway would not follow me," he said. "One day, perhaps, but not now. Besides, there is Magnus."

"King Olaf once said to me that you would live to rule over Norway . . ." began Helgi, and then he stopped as he remembered the rest of the king's saying: that Harald would die a violent death in a foreign land. "Your time will come," he concluded.

"Yes," replied Harald, "my time will come." Then suddenly, to Helgi's astonishment, he covered his face with his hands and began to weep.

"Why," said Helgi, much taken aback, for he had never known his old playmate give way to tears before, "what ails you, Harald? You must have patience and your turn will come."

"Don't be a fool," sniffed Harald, rubbing his sleeve across his eyes. "Do you think I care about that? It's just that . . . well, he is my brother and I was hoping . . . well, never mind. He is my king, too, isn't he? What can you, an Icelander, know of such things?"

"I think that perhaps we have all been living too much on hopes," replied Helgi quietly. "In the spring I shall travel to Holmgarth, whatever the others may say."

"And I shall come with you," said Harald. And now that they had decided, the two boys were more cheerful, though they chafed and grumbled at the slow passing of the time, watching impatiently for the first signs of a thaw and the coming of warmer weather.

Then one day a ship put into the mouth of the river below Sarpsborg, although the ice was still thick at the banks. It was a merchant vessel from the island of Gotland in the Eastern Sea, and its crew reported that King Olaf of Norway had lately come to their island with a fleet out of Holmgarth, heading westward to Sweden. He had questioned the folk in Gotland closely about events in Norway, and had learned from them—as the people of Sarpsborg learned, too, for the first time—that Earl Hakon Ericsson had been lost at sea that winter off the coast of Scotland, and that Norway was now without a chief.

At once, said the Gotlander, King Olaf had ordered his ships to put to sea, and doubtless by this time he and his men were in Sweden. It was not certain, the man concluded, that his errand was a peaceful one.

This news set the little Norwegian township in an uproar. All those who had fled from their estates because of Earl Hakon and the other minions of the Danish king now began to get ready to join King Olaf in Sweden. Word was sent to Tunsberg and all those parts of eastern Norway about the Oslofjord, where the people were still sympathetic toward the family of Harald Fairhair, and both men and supplies were gathered for an expedition.

The question was, what did the king intend? Would he march through southern Sweden to join up with them there, where his support was likely to be strongest; or would he put to sea and sail up into the fjord from the south; or was he planning an invasion of Norway across the mountains, with the help of the Swedes, into the heart of the Tronderlaw where the heathen opposition against his rule was centered?

Messengers were at once sent into Sweden under armed escort to get information, while the Norwegians at Sarpsborg sharpened their axes and swords and watched the sea anxiously in case the Danes should have heard something. King Knut was said to be in England, but no one knew what his son Hardiknut might be doing, for he was in Denmark at this time.

Harald and Helgi both begged to go with the messengers to the king, but they were forbidden to leave the garth. Harald's safety was too important to the loyal chieftains, they told him, for he was next in line for the kingship if King Olaf and his son Magnus fell into the hands of their enemies. "As for the young Icelander," they said, "how can we tell that he will not betray us to the Danes, like Sigvat, his countryman?"

Harald tried bribing some of the guards who watched the gate to let them out of the garth, but without success. Then one night he and Helgi made up their minds to break out over the high palisade. Taking some money with them, and food that they had stolen from the kitchens, they found a place where one of the storehouses leaned up against the wooden palings, and managed to get up onto the roof. From the top of the palisade it was a drop almost twice the height of a man, but there was deep snow underneath and they landed safely.

They were free.

After that, it was just a matter of walking until they came to a place where they could buy horses; but they

dared not take the northward road into Sweden for fear
of being followed and brought back, and the forest tracks
that, according to Harald, led more directly across the
border to the east, were deep in snow.

For the whole of that night they floundered through
drifts that sometimes reached to their waists, until daylight found them lying exhausted in the shelter of a deserted forester's cabin.

No snow had fallen since they left Sarpsborg, so it was
not difficult for Thord Folason and others of the guard
on skis to catch up with them and bring them back the
same day to the royal garth.

"You'll be lucky if they don't put you back in the jailhouse after this, Helgi *minn*," said Thord.

Thanks to Harald, Helgi was spared this final shame,
though both of them were made to promise that they
would not try to get out again. Tempers were short among
the chieftains, and even Harald's rank, they told him,
would not save him and his companion from fetters unless they agreed to give their word; so they did so.

Shortly before Easter the messengers returned from
Sweden. They had been able to make contact with some
of King Olaf's men there, and had learned that the king
was in the north of Sweden with Queen Astrid and a
Swedish chieftain of Norwegian family named Dag
Ringsson, who was helping them to raise an army. The
king of Sweden had refused to help openly, but had
freely given leave for any Swede to join them if he
wished.

By this time there was a force of about six hundred
fighting men gathered at Sarpsborg. They were without
a leader and without a plan, for there was none among

them who did not regard himself as the equal of any other. Nevertheless it was agreed at a house-*thing* that the best course would be to join King Olaf without delay, for the reports suggested that he was planning an invasion of Norway across the mountains.

And so the six hundred set off into Sweden, through the dark forests that stretched like a sea before them. And Harald, who was then fifteen years of age, and his friend Helgi the Icelander, went with them, both eager to fight their first battle for King Olaf and Norway. They had been told, too, that they would be fighting for the Christian Faith, to drive back all the old, evil powers that were springing up once more in the land—Bishop Grimkel had sent them his personal blessing—though Helgi found it strange that to do this they would be calling upon the heathen Swedes for help.

It was a cold, weary march through the forests, but the spirits of the little army were buoyed up by hope and enthusiasm. On their passage through the Swedish district of Vermaland they were joined by a few Norwegians who had fled across the border. The Swedes regarded them with a mixture of fear and hostility but, when they showed their willingness to pay for provisions and horses, traded with them and let them pass in peace.

They caught up with the main body of the king's army in the sparsely inhabited region of Jarnberaland, where he had set up camp beside the road to the north. Their high spirits were a little dashed when they saw that his force was not much larger than their own, but King Olaf welcomed them and embraced his brother Harald warmly.

"I have not deserved such loyalty," he said, and those

who were near him said that there were tears in his eyes.

Helgi held back at this first meeting, though he longed to be spoken to by the king. A strange, paralyzing kind of shyness seemed to overwhelm him. Would the king even remember who he was? For fear that he might not and that he would be shamed before his companions, he busied himself among the baggage horses until the king had withdrawn into his tent. While he was occupied in this way, a familiar voice hailed him, and he looked up to see his uncle Thorarin standing before him.

"Habit is like an old wound, eh, Helgi *minn?*" said Thorarin with a grin. "Long after it's healed, it itches, and you can't but scratch it to save your life. So here we are, an old fool and a young one, and which is the bigger fool of us I cannot say."

The King's Return

"It was a bitter winter," said Thormod the Scald. "The worst I have known, and I have been in Greenland, too. The nights in Holmgarth were ever full of the howling of wolves and of the wind in forests that seemed to go on to the end of the world."

Helgi shuddered and drew closer to the fire. They were

camped in a sheltered valley in Jamtland, a wild upland area of northern Sweden, where the howl of wolves in the forest was not unknown, even in early summer. Behind them lay many days of riding and tramping along forest tracks. Ahead stretched the empty highlands that separated Sweden from Norway, where giants and trolls were said to share their caves with the bears and the mountain eagles, and where wayfarers sought the protection of saints and angels against the powers of darkness.

"Tell us about the country of the *Russ*, Thormod," said one of the Norwegians.

"I am an exile from my own land," continued Thormod, "but here in Sweden, and in Norway and Denmark, and in parts of England, too, I can speak my own tongue and men will understand me. But there are whole regions of Holmgarth, away from the cities and trading settlements of the Swedish *Russ*, where the people speak a wild, barbaric tongue that is not like human speech at all, but more like the mumblings and incantations of Finnish wizards. With King Olaf in Holmgarth I felt an exile from my own kind."

"And yet I have heard it said that the king of the *Russ* held King Olaf in great honor," said Helgi.

"Not only King Yaroslav and his queen, but all the people, too," replied Thormod. He glanced over his shoulder before continuing. One of the guard was leaning on his spear outside the king's tent less than thirty paces away. Thormod lowered his voice and said, "Strange tales have been told about the king."

"What sort of tales?" asked a thickset, bearded man beside him.

"The king will not have any speak of such things, Dag

Ringsson," replied Thormod, "but I must tell you that he has changed much since he went from Norway. He spends much time of a night in prayer—more than ever before. And men say . . . it is said that he does miracles."

"Miracles?" said Dag Ringsson, raising his eyebrows. "He'll need a few now to win the support of his people. Can he draw down thunder and lightning, as the old magicians did?"

"Not that kind of miracle," said Thormod. "Once, in the city of King Yaroslav, a noble woman brought her son to the queen. He was about twelve years old and he had a terrible swelling in his throat so that he could swallow neither food nor drink, and the doctors had given up all hope of saving him. Well, it seems that the queen said, 'Go to King Olaf, the Norwegian. He is the best doctor here in the land. Bid him do what he can for your boy.' And the woman did so."

"And what did King Olaf do?" asked Helgi. He was sitting on the other side of Thormod, his knees drawn up under his chin and the hood of his sheepskin *ulpa* pulled forward over his face.

"The king told her that he was not a doctor, and that she should go to one. But she still begged him to do what he could for the boy, and at last he agreed to have a look at him, and went to his bedside. He made the boy open his mouth and then he thrust his fingers down his throat and worked at the swelling. After that he took a piece of bread, broke it, and laid it in the palm of his hand in the form of a cross. Then he put the fragments in the boy's mouth and made him swallow, and almost at once the swelling disappeared, and after a few days the boy was quite well again."

"Was that a miracle?" asked Helgi doubtfully.

"Everyone said it was," replied Thormod. "But the king gets very angry when he hears men speak of it, for he says that it was only God's power working through common sense, and that he is the last person through whom God would choose to do a miracle.

"It is strange how much he seems to punish himself sometimes," Thormod continued. "I remember once he was sitting by the fire on a Sunday evening. You know what a craftsman he is with his hands, and how he dislikes at all times to be idle. Well, that evening as he sat there, he had taken a piece of wood in his hand and was whittling at it with his sheath knife. I thought nothing of this, but it seems that he had told one of the pages to warn him if, through his forgetfulness, he ever did anything against the Church's Law. But he still has a hasty temper, and the boy was afraid to speak straight out, so he said, 'Lord, remember that it is Monday tomorrow.'

"The king looked at him and then looked down at the knife in his hand, and saw that he had been working on the Lord's day. At once he swept all the chips of wood on the floor in front of him into a heap and gathered them into the palm of his hand. Then he bade the page take a brand from the fire and set light to the chips, and he sat there without flinching while they burned in his open hand, though his eyes were filled with tears of pain."

"Why should the king wish to punish himself?" said Helgi. "I think that he is a better Christian than any of us here, and I know that I have done worse than whittle a piece of wood on the Lord's day."

"Perhaps I can tell you part of the answer to that question," said Thormod. "You have heard how Bjorn the Marshal came back to the king?"

"He came, as I did, and my uncle Thorarin, and many others, when we heard that the king would try to win back Norway and that he needed us," said Helgi.

"No, it was before that," said Thormod. "It was Yuletide, and the snow lay deep on the ground in all Holmgarth when Bjorn arrived with a party of horsemen at the royal palace. He threw himself at King Olaf's feet and said, 'I put myself in God's hands and yours, my king. I have accepted gifts from Knut's men and I have sworn oaths of loyalty to him, but as long as you live, and I live too, I shall follow you and never leave you.'

"At this the king's face went red and he put a hand on Bjorn's shoulder and said, 'Get up, Bjorn. I forgive you, if there is anything for me to forgive. It is with God that you must make your peace. I know, however, that if you have failed me, loyal as you are, then there cannot be many in Norway still faithful to me; and for this I am much to blame, for I have deserted my trust and failed in my duty to God, leaving my people to suffer the violence of my enemies.'

"It was soon after this that the king made up his mind that he must go back to Norway. Everyone told him that it would be madness, with every hand turned against him and the men of Earl Hakon and King Knut sitting armed and ready in the land. King Yaroslav offered him a kingdom over the Bulgars if he would stay there in his dominions, but he would not accept. He said that he had thought of going to Jerusalem and entering a monastery, but then he had dreamed a dream as he lay on his couch in his own chamber one night."

"The king has spoken to me of this dream of his," said a voice behind them, and Thormod and Helgi both looked round to see Thorarin Nefjolfsson standing there in the light of the fire.

"He spoke to me of this dream," repeated Thorarin, "because it was like another dream he had once, many years ago."

"When he turned back from Spain?" asked Helgi.

"The same," replied his uncle, "for it seemed to him that a tall, fair man in fine clothes came and stood by his couch, and it was the man who had come to him before, and he said, 'Why are you so uneasy in your mind, Olaf? It is strange that you should be wondering whether or not to accept a fief from a foreign king and give up the crown and title which God alone gave you. Do not fear what those about you say. Go back to the kingdom which you inherited and which you have long ruled with the help of God. It is a king's duty to defeat his enemies, and his death will be an honorable one if he falls in battle at the side of his men.'

"It was at that moment," said Thorarin, "that the king awakened, and he thought that he caught a glimpse of a man going out of his chamber, and he is certain that this man was his kinsman, King Olaf Tryggvason, who died at the hands of his enemies thirty years ago."

There was a long silence when Thorarin finished speaking. Then Thormod said, "It is true that many spoke against this expedition from the start, but I, for one, would rather die beside King Olaf than live out my life in exile; and besides, I think that luck will be with us and that God will help the king, who has served Him so well."

"Let us not talk of dying," said Dag Ringsson. "We shall win back Norway for the king, and live to enjoy our victory."

King Olaf's army numbered about twelve hundred men in all when it marched north from Jamtland, including two hundred who had followed him all the way to Holmgarth and back. The Norwegians from Sarpsborg had joined up with some exiled fellow countrymen who had been with Queen Astrid in Sweden and had been put under the command of the Norwegian-Swedish chieftain, Dag Ringsson. In addition, there was a force of Swedish volunteers—mostly men who had joined the king's standard for loot or love of fighting. These formed a separate body under their own leaders. The royal guard—nearly all of them among the faithful two hundred who had accompanied the king into exile—remained under King Olaf's own command, with Bjorn the Marshal as his lieutenant and Thord Folason as standard-bearer. These were the men who had taken an oath never to leave the king, except at his order, and to die on the field of battle rather than give way to his enemies. The membership of this chosen band was a jealously guarded privilege, and Helgi was filled with envy when he saw Harald, a few days after they had joined the king, wearing the bearskin jacket of a guardsman.

"Now it seems that you are enjoying the benefit of being the king's brother," he remarked rather acidly; but Harald laughed and replied that on the battlefield it was not certain that his relationship would be any protection to him.

"Your kinsman Thorarin belongs to the guard because of his old friendship with King Olaf," he added. "Why don't you ask him to speak to the king for you? I shall do the same, if you wish it."

Helgi had himself only once spoken to the king since he had reached Sweden. It had been on the evening of their arrival, when Thorarin had taken him to the king's tent and left him there.

It had seemed to Helgi that King Olaf had aged; for all that he was no more than thirty-five, there were already gray streaks in the red-brown of his hair and beard. He looked serene, though, and filled with peace, more like a man about to set out on a journey to visit old friends than a deposed king who was on the point of marching into the heart of a hostile country.

"You are the Icelandic boy, aren't you?" he had said when Helgi knelt to kiss his hand. "You should have stayed in Iceland. Our quarrels are no concern of yours. You were wrong to leave your family."

"My father is better, lord," Helgi had replied boldly. "My kinsman Thorarin Nefjolfsson is come all this way to serve you, so why not I?"

"Thorarin is an old friend and his case is different," said the king. "Besides," he continued with a smile, "do you know what he said when I told him that he was too old for fighting and ought to sail his ship back home again? He said, 'I have never been much of a hero when it came to fighting, king, and it may be that I am both older and uglier than I used to be. As for sailing my ship back home again, well, the truth is that I am becoming weary of the sea. I think I shall come with you to Norway.'"

"I am weary of minding sheep and mowing hay," said Helgi.

"Better a live shepherd than a dead hero," replied the king.

"I am sixteen years old," said Helgi. "Your brother Harald is younger."

"Do you know me so little," said the king, frowning, "that you have not learned to obey? You Icelanders are a proud, self-willed people. . . ."

"Strike me dead if you will, king," said Helgi, his voice scarcely raised above a whisper, "but let me come with you."

Then the king had gazed at him for a moment with those fierce blue eyes that seemed to pierce a man to his innermost soul and, after a while, he had begun to laugh, saying, "It would be a troublesome business, taking you with me, if I were to strike you dead, boy. You had better come with me alive, since that is what you want. But remember, it will not be too late to turn back at any time."

After they left Jarnberaland, marching northward through the forests, the king had ridden at the head of the column, which was spread out along the track for more than a mile by daytime. It was only at night, when the army camped under the protection of outlying pickets, that Helgi saw anything of him or his closer companions. Then he would gaze enviously at the members of the guard, distinguished by the bearskin cloaks worn over their ring mail, who talked and joked freely with the king as with a familiar friend.

Each morning before the army moved off, Mass would be said in front of the king's tent by one of the priests

who accompanied him—Master Geir was not one of them,
for he had left Norway to preach the Faith to the heathen
folk of Jutland—and all but some of the Swedes, and
others who were not Christians, would stand devoutly with
their weapons in their hands until the ceremony was
over. After that the king would hold a brief council with
the leaders and hear reports from the spies who had been
sent on ahead under cover of darkness, and finally the
war horn would be sounded as a signal for the army to
march.

One day Helgi had just taken his place in the second
hundred of the Norwegian force and they were waiting
for Dag Ringsson to return from the council of leaders,
when the king himself passed by. He saw Helgi and
stopped in front of him.

"Helgi the Icelander," he said, "I have been wanting
to speak with you. I would not have it thought by any-
one that King Olaf does not know how to show gratitude
when men go out of their way to serve him."

"I have been well paid, lord," replied Helgi, "by your
allowing me to stay with you."

"Some would call that poor payment," said the king,
"and I think that I owe you more than this. You may
choose a gift, whatever is in my power at this time to
give, and it shall be yours."

"Then my choice is easily made, lord," said Helgi, falling on his knee.

"Well?" said the king. "Remember that if you ask for
land or a chief's name, these things are in the hand of
God alone to give, as things are at present."

"I want neither land nor chieftaincy," replied Helgi.
"Let me be a member of your guard, king."

The king raised his eyebrows at this. Then he turned and called for Bjorn the Marshal, who came hurrying forward, redder in the face and stouter than ever.

"Here is Helgi, come all the way from Iceland, and it seems that he will be satisfied with nothing less than to become a member of the guard," said the king.

Bjorn went almost purple and seemed to have difficulty in speaking.

"That boy . . ." he spluttered, "never fought a battle . . . seasoned warriors . . . too young . . ."

"Bjorn," said the king, "I was two years younger than he when I helped Ethelred of England take London Bridge from the Danes."

"You were only twelve years old when you went on your first viking expedition, lord," said a voice beside him, and Helgi saw his uncle Thorarin there, looking strangely out of place in his bearskin and steel cap. "I will answer for the boy," he added.

"So will I," said Thormod the Scald, coming up behind him.

"And I, too," said Harald, who was with Thormod.

"You see, Bjorn." The king laughed. "We shall have to take him whether we like it or not."

Bjorn the Marshal snorted indignantly, but he signed to Helgi to follow him to the guards' bivouac to be instructed in the duties of the king's chosen companions.

The next morning, on the shores of a great lake on the high plateau between Norway and Sweden, after they had heard Mass, Helgi walked forward between his two sponsors, Thormod and Thorarin, and took the guardsman's oath, standing before the army. When he had been blessed by the priest, the king gave him a sword to wear.

"Lord," said Helgi, "if I were Thormod, or Sigvat, or even your kinsman Harald, then maybe I would make a verse in your honor to thank you for the sword-gift. But I have no skill in that art."

"Use the sword truly, in my service and the defense of our Holy Faith," replied the king. "Such will be better thanks than verses."

After this, Helgi rode with the king's force at the head of the column. When a day or two had passed, he noticed that the track had begun to slope downward ahead of them and they were entering a narrow valley with steep, pine-covered mountain walls to either side of them. Thorarin told him that they were in Norway and were coming into Veradale.

"By this way we shall enter Trondheim from the north, whence we are least expected," he said. "The king means to strike at his enemies in the heart of their own country, for the people of these parts ever held more by Earl Eric and Earl Hakon than by the king, and were more for their heathen customs of old times than for the new learning."

"But both of the earls are now dead," said Helgi, "and all the folk of the Tronderlaw have accepted King Olaf and the true Faith these many years past, or so Master Geir has told me."

"There is an old saying in Iceland," replied Thorarin, "that fire lives long in ancient ashes. We shall soon find out what sort of a welcome the men of Trondheim have in store for their king."

It was about this time that men began to notice a

change in the king. Usually he was of a gay and lively humor, talking much with those about him and making men laugh with his sallies; but of late he had become silent and had taken to riding alone, and if any approached to speak with him on matters of importance he would answer shortly; while at the council of leaders his mind would often seem to be far away. Some of the chief men of the army became worried at this, fearing that his mood would have an ill effect on the rest, and they persuaded one of the chaplains to speak with him about it. Helgi was behind Bjorn the Marshal, with Thormod and Harald, when the priest went up to the king who was riding some thirty paces ahead of them, and they watched the two men anxiously, prepared for a sudden explosion of wrath and the hasty retreat of the priest. But after a while he turned back toward them, his face clouded by an expression of wonder—almost of fear.

"What did he say?" asked Bjorn. "Has he lost heart or heard bad news?"

The priest shook his head. "I can hardly tell what to say," he replied. "The king speaks strangely. God has shown him a wonder, but of its meaning I am greatly in doubt."

"What wonder?" asked Thormod. "Tell us what he said."

"He said these words," replied the priest: "'As I looked westward from the mountains, I saw Norway before me, and I thought how many happy days I had spent in that land. And then it was as if I could see the whole of Trondheim at once, and after that all Norway, and then further still, until at last the whole world lay before me, both land and sea.'"

The priest paused and looked at his hearers.

"Go on," said Thormod. "What then?"

"The king said, 'All those places to which I had been in my lifetime, I recognized clearly. Others, of which I had but heard and even those which were quite strange to me, both desert and inhabited land, I knew also, to the ends of the world.'"

"What can such a vision mean?" asked Thormod with a frown. "That all Trondheim will be his, and then all Norway, and that his fame, like that of Charlemagne, will reach to the ends of the earth?"

"It must be so," said Helgi eagerly. "What do you say, Master Bjorn?"

Bjorn snorted. "I say that this is no time for visions," he replied. "Such things are well enough in times of peace, but it is in my mind that the king will soon have other things to think of."

Not long after this, the valley down which they were advancing began to broaden out before them, and the army divided in three parts, each force, under its leader, taking a separate track. The king with his standard and the guard took the middle way along the bank of a river. Already they had passed outlying settlements, and soon they came to meadows and cornfields.

"Let every man take care not to trample the corn," the king warned those about him, and word was passed back along the line. But a few of the rear guard, who had lagged behind with pack horses carrying stores and baggage, had become separated from the main force. These men did not hear the king's warning, and they cut across the cornfields to catch up with their comrades and trampled the corn as they went.

That evening, when the guard had set up camp beside the river and the evening meal was being prepared over crackling wood fires, a man and two boys were brought in by one of the pickets, who said that they had been found hanging about nearby. The man demanded to speak with the king, and so the captives were taken to Bjorn the Marshal, who led them to the king's tent. The boys were silent and sullen-looking, but the man, a short, stocky fellow with a peasant's large, knotted hands, bristled with indignation.

"My corn is ruined," he spluttered, "trampled flat by those bungling berserks of yours. . . . A fine way to treat a loyal Norwegian."

"You are speaking to the king," said Bjorn, shocked.

"Of course I am," replied the man. "I'd be wasting my time else."

"Who are you, fellow, that speak so boldly?" asked the king. "Do you not know that your life is in danger?"

"I know that my livelihood is, as I have said before. My name is Thorgeir and I am the farmer whose fields you have trampled," replied the man. "You will find little joy among the farmers of Trondheim if you have come to spoil their crops, king."

"Have no fear, Thorgeir," said King Olaf. "You will be paid the full value of the crops that have been damaged, out of my treasure chest, and it may be that your corn will grow none the worse because my men have trampled it. But tell me now what tidings there are of happenings in Norway, and whether I may expect to meet with any strength of arms raised against me."

Thorgeir looked grave at this and replied, "I have heard that the news of your coming has spread to every part of Norway, king, and that many chiefs are come here, both from the south and from Halogaland in the north, and a mighty army is being gathered in Trondheim against you. But whether they intend to come to meet you or to wait for you down by the fjord, I cannot say."

"I think that you are an honest man, Thorgeir," said the king. "What do the people say of me and my coming?"

The farmer looked at the ground at his feet. Then he said, "I have heard men speak, some one way and some another. There are some who say that they are better off without a king to tell them what they should do and believe, where their fathers were free to follow the old customs. Others say that it may now be seen what sort of a king they have been able to rid themselves of, that comes with a foreign army to plunder and ravage the land, and many of them heathen Swedes and their ancient foes. Again there are others who complain of the taxes laid upon them by the Danes, and the violence and lawlessness of the chiefs, now that there is no king in the land."

"You have spoken freely, Thorgeir," said the king, "and I am grateful to you. Now tell me what boys these two are with you, that have such a determined look about them."

"These are my sons, king," replied Thorgeir. "They want to join your army."

"They are too young," said the king. "This is no viking

raid which we are going on, but a grim war in which many will be left dead on the field of battle."

"I have told them so," said the farmer, "but they will not take a refusal."

"How is this?" said the king. "They must be made to obey. You, boy"—he addressed the elder of the two—"you are to stay with your father, do you hear?"

"Yes, lord," replied the boy.

"You will stay, then?" said the king.

"No, lord," replied the boy. "I mean that I hear you, but I will not stay, nor will my brother."

The king's brow descended in a scowl like a thundercloud, but Helgi, who had been standing by the entrance of the tent, could see that there was a twinkle in his eye.

"Bjorn," said the king. "What are we to do about them?"

"Let us bind them with ropes, lord," replied the marshal. "In this way they will be made to stay, whether they will or no."

The king shook his head and smiled.

"If they are sent away now, they will come back later," he said. "It will be less trouble for us if we let them have what they want. They must stay with the baggage train, though, when battle is joined. Helgi, take these boys to Dag Ringsson and bid him find them employment."

The two boys followed Helgi with admiring glances at his guardsman's bearskin and long sword as he led them by a woodland path to the encampment of the main Norwegian force.

"Why are you wearing that thing," asked the younger of them; "in the heat of the summer, too?"

"I am one of the guard," said Helgi lightly, but inwardly almost bursting with pride. "We are they who fight next to the king in battle."

The boy digested this information thoughtfully. "Hmm," he grunted, "I think that you should find the work there warm enough."

"Why have you made up your minds to join King Olaf?" asked Helgi, slightly ruffled. "You need expect nothing but wounds and danger in his service. You would have done better to stay with your father on the farm, as he told you."

"We are tired of being ordered about by our father," replied the elder boy. "Besides, our neighbor at Staf has three sons, and they have all gone to join the chieftains' army, or so we have heard. We would not have them boasting over us for the rest of our lives."

After he had left the farmer's sons with Dag Ringsson, Helgi was making his way back to the king's bivouac when he walked into a patrol of the guard returning up the valley. It was led by Finn Arnason, who asked him eagerly where the king was to be found.

"We have grave news for him," he said. "The chieftains have assembled a great army, the like of which has never before been seen in Norway, and they are less than a day's march away, at the northern end of the Trondheimsfjord."

Sticklestead

The news was serious. Most of the king's followers had
hoped that there would be some fighting and looting,
for the love of it and the leveling of old scores; but none
had expected organized opposition on the scale suggested by Finn Arnason.

"I had thought that the people of Norway would flock

to the king's standard to throw off their Danish tyrants," exclaimed Thormod when he heard the report.

But Thorarin said, "No doubt the common people would welcome him back, but they fear the rough handling that they might get from their own chieftains. The poor have little to lose, but the rich and powerful are ever the enemies of change."

"Then we should give the people something that would make them yet more afraid of us," said Finn Arnason grimly.

If the king felt either fear or disappointment at Finn's news, he showed neither.

"God will give us the victory, for our cause is right," he said simply. But his face darkened with anger and sorrow when he was told what men were the leaders of the chieftains' army. They were none other than Thorir Hound, his trusted liegeman of Halogaland, and Calf Arnason, who had been a member of the guard and his friend.

"Now I understand why Finn is so bitter," said Thorarin, "since his own brother has turned traitor."

"His younger brother, Thorberg, is with us, though," said Helgi.

"The Arnasons were always among the foremost of the king's men," said Thorarin. They were seated round a fire a few paces from the king's tent in the still brightness of the northern summer night.

"It was a mortal blow to the king when he heard the news," said Thormod the Scald. "Did you see his face?"

"Severe, but not mortal," said Thorarin. "He has learned that a king must stand alone and not lean too heavily upon his friends."

"With Thorir Hound it is what might be expected," Thormod continued. "But Calf . . ."

"Did not Thorir take an oath as the king's liegeman?" asked Helgi. "Is honor not to be expected among the Halogalanders?"

"You have not heard what happened to his kinsman, Asbjorn Sealsbane," replied Thormod. "It was the autumn when you and Thorarin sailed for Iceland, I believe."

"What happened?" asked Helgi. "I know that Asbjorn took an oath to serve the king as bailiff at Avaldsness, in place of the man named Seal-Thorir, whom he killed, and I heard that he went back home to the north and did not return at the agreed time."

"He did not return, ever," said Thormod, "and one of the king's servants, a man named Carl, went north after him. You remember what a fellow Asbjorn was for fine clothing? Well, one day they came across his ship in a fjord, and there he was, dressed like a courtier, at the helm. Carl's companion said, 'That is Sealsbane at the steering oar, in a blue kirtle.' Carl replied, 'I'll give him a red kirtle!' and with that he hurled a spear that pinned Asbjorn Sealsbane to the gunnel of his own ship."

"It can't be said that his fate was undeserved," remarked Helgi. "What happened to Carl?"

"He died by the spear that pierced Sealsbane," replied Thormod. "But that was not the end of the matter, for when the mother of Sealsbane went to Thorir Hound, her brother-in-law, and handed him the spear, saying, 'It was your fault, Thorir, that my son met his death, and I name you every man's coward if you don't avenge him—when she said this, Thorir took the matter much to heart and determined not only to slay Carl, as he did,

but also to get even with King Olaf, who put this shame
on his family."

"That is not difficult to understand," said Helgi, "especially as I have heard that Thorir Hound was ever a
man like Erling of Rogaland, who took it hard that he
must bend the knee to a king—"

"He is not alone in that, among the Norwegian chieftains," muttered Thorarin.

"—But that Calf, who was the king's close friend—"

"Who can say what a man will do for wealth and
power?" interrupted Thormod, glancing across at Bjorn
the Marshal, who had at this minute come from the king's
tent.

"What ails you, Bjorn?" asked Thorarin. "You look as
though you have eaten something sour that has turned
your stomach."

Bjorn glared at the three of them as if they were to
blame for some great wrong. *Could he have heard the
words of Thormod?* wondered Helgi. But then the marshal said, "It might well be as you say, Thorarin, seeing
that the king appears to have gone out of his mind. We
hear that a great army is arrayed to meet us in the
Tronderlaw, and the king commands that every heathen
among us must now either receive baptism or leave his
standard."

"You are joking," exclaimed Thormod. "More than half
the Swedes are Frey-worshipers, and there are more than
a few among the Norwegians under Dag Ringsson who
are not baptized."

"So I have told the king," replied Bjorn, "and his
answer to me was that we should not trust in numbers.
He said, 'We shall trust in God, for our victory will rest

upon His power and His mercy, but I shall have no heathen man in my army.'"

The following day a crowd of men, both Norwegian and Swedish received baptism from the priests on the bank of the river. But Helgi learned that about four hundred heathens had chosen to return home and had left the army.

Harald, the king's brother, received this news cheerfully.

"Christian or heathen, it's all one to me," he said. "The fewer the men, the greater the glory."

"For those that live to see the end of the day of battle, maybe," remarked Thorarin dryly. "For my part, I would as soon share the glory with a larger force and have more hope of enjoying it."

It seemed that even the king must have felt some sympathy for this view, for he allowed Bjorn to send men into the surrounding country to raise levies and commandeer supplies, only insisting that no man should join his standard who was not a baptized Christian or willing to accept the Faith.

But the men who had been sent out returned with reports of little success. Many of the farmers had joined the army of the chieftains; others had refused to take up arms against him whom they regarded as their lawful king but were unwilling to fight against their own kinsfolk and friends. When the king called a council to decide what should be done, Finn Arnason spoke out boldly, and Helgi, on the fringe of the *thing*, heard him call out for the punishment of the faithless peasants.

"Let us harry the countryside," he cried. "Let us plunder and burn, so that not a farm nor a cottage is left

standing. Besides," he added, "it may be that when the
farmers see the smoke from their homesteads and wonder what has happened to their womenfolk and children
and old people, then they will be tempted to leave the
ranks of the chieftains."

There was much applause at this, but the king held
up his hand for silence and said, "I have punished men
harshly when they have offended against God and
sacrificed to idols; but in this they have offended against
me and are therefore less worthy of such punishment."

There was a murmur of protest at this, but the king
continued, "It may be, even now, that the chieftains will
agree to terms and make peace with me. If they do not,
burned farms and slaughtered cattle will be of little profit
to any man, win or lose."

"Ay, that is true," said Bjorn. "If any are hoping for
lands or loot, they would do well to think of it."

"Besides this," continued the king, "these are my
people, and whatever faults they may be guilty of, it is
my wish that you behave discreetly and commit no out-
rage. If you catch any spies, though, they shall be put to
death."

That same day the army crossed over the river by a
ford, leaving behind all the pack horses and baggage and
such men as were not to be in the fighting; among them
the priests and those set to guard the king's treasure
chest and the other stores. The king would have made
his half brother Harald stay behind, saying that he was
too young to fight, but the boy blankly refused, and for
once the king gave way, though he bade Thorarin watch
over him to see that he came to no harm.

That evening about sunset they came to a place where

the valley opened out a little between wooded slopes, and they could see a line of water gleaming in the distance with blue mountains beyond.

"There's the fjord," said Harald, and Helgi, who was beside him, remarked, "I know this place. I have been here before." He gave a little shiver as he looked about him, in spite of the warmth of the summer evening. There was a group of low farm buildings away to their left under the hillside.

"What homestead is that?" he asked Finn Arnason.

"Sticklestead," replied Finn, "and unless I am mistaken, that is the farmer, Thorgils Halmuson, coming to meet us."

"You remember, Harald?" said Helgi. "We came here once, in the wintertime, and the sky was dark and it was cold, with a howling of wolves."

"Did we? I don't know," replied Harald absently. "I wonder what the farmer wants with us."

"To save his skin, I dare wager," said Finn.

But it seemed that Thorgils had come to offer his services to the king, for he was armed with sword and spear, and with him he brought some men who carried staves and reaping hooks. He spoke for some time with the king, who was on foot now at the head of the column, but after a while Helgi saw him turn back with his companions and return to his farm, carrying a leather bag in one hand.

Thormod the Scald, who had been up with the king, now came back with orders for the leaders, and he told Helgi that the farmer had been commanded to return to his home and look after the wounded after the battle, and bury the dead, and the king had given him silver for Masses to be said for all that died there.

"But I may not stand here gossiping with you, boy," he said. "The army is to be drawn up in order of battle at once, for the enemy is on the road from the fjord and less than an hour's march from Sticklestead."

"It will not be long before you have a taste of fighting, boys," said Finn when Helgi told him and Harald the news.

"The sooner the better," said Harald grimly.

Helgi felt a little sick in his stomach, and he swallowed and remarked, "At least it will be an end to this traveling."

"No, you will not have to travel far now," said Finn. "A guardsman does not flee, nor leave his master on the field of battle."

"No, but he may have to chase after the enemy," said Harald. "Listen, I have made a verse."

"Not now," said Finn. "The signal is given for the army to gather about the king."

The king was standing on a small hillock near the track, with Bjorn and other leaders near him. The forces were now drawn up in a half ring before him in the meadows, and he spoke to them.

It was a lovely, still, clear summer evening. The red glow of the sunset had not yet faded from the wooded slopes above the valley, and the king's voice rang out distinctly, so that every man could hear his words.

"I have chosen this place in which to give battle to the traitors," he announced. "Here we have a great and fair army, and this is how I intend to dispose it. In the center, on this hill where I am now standing, I shall set up my standard, with my guard and those men from the Tronderlaw who have joined us. Dag Ringsson will be on the right with the Norwegians who have come with us from Sweden, while the Swedes will be on the left, above the farm. Every force will have its own standard and will be divided into troops under chosen leaders, so that each man will fight beside his kinsmen and friends. You shall rally to your standards in the battle, and from this time none must leave his standard or his troop and all must be fully armed, night and day, for we do not know when the attack will come. And let every man mark his helmet and his shield with the Holy Cross as a war token. And when battle is joined, let this be our watchword and rallying cry: 'Forward, Christ's men, Cross men, king's men!' "

At this the whole army took up the cry and beat on their shields with their weapons, and a flock of ravens flew up from the woods above them and circled overhead, calling harshly.

"The birds of Odin are gathered for the feast," declared Thormod the Scald.

The king heard his words and frowned angrily. Then his brow cleared and he said with a smile, "As a poet, Thormod, you may say such a thing without rebuke; but you would be wiser to think upon the saints and holy angels who are gathered to protect us."

"That may be so, lord," replied Thormod boldly. "We Icelanders are given to speaking what is in our minds. But at least," he added with a touch of malice, "it is something that you have *one* scald to stand by you at this time." And with that he recited a verse that was obviously aimed at his rival, the absent Sigvat:

"Till another scald has filled,
king, bold in battle-*thing*,
(are you expecting him soon?)
my place, I shall bide by your side.
One will not fail: we shall win
and feed our foes to the raven,
or else, sea-rover, ourselves
lie cold and stark on the mold.

"And I don't know where he to whom you once gave a gold-hilted sword is now," he added, "but I know that my only wish is to stay by your side."

"There is no need to blame Sigvat," said the king. "He is on a pilgrimage and thinking of his soul's good, and would want to be with us now if he knew how things were. But this one thing I promise you, Thormod, and that is that you and I will not be parted, whatever happens on the morrow."

After this the king's army took up its battle positions and the men lay down where they were, fully armed, to rest, while pickets were sent out to give warning of the enemy.

Helgi and Harald lay down near the king with Thorarin, Finn Arnason and his brother Thorberg, Bjorn and Thormod the Scald. The king himself was a little apart from the others and he sat with his cloak about him, hands clasped round his knees, and gazed down the valley from which the chieftains' army would approach.

Helgi dozed but woke late in the night, though it was still twilight and only two or three of the brightest stars winked in the summer sky. He felt cold and stiff, and when he turned to find a more comfortable place he could see the king, still in the same position, and it seemed to him that he was praying, for his lips were moving. Nearby Thormod lay stretched out on the ground in deep sleep.

After that, Helgi dozed off again, and when he awoke, the sun was beginning to rise, for he could see the fjord shining like fire down in the valley. The king was still sitting up, but now he was talking to Thormod the Scald.

"It is early yet," Helgi heard him say. "Give me a poem, Thormod, to pass the time away."

The Darkening of the Sun

Thormod the Scald sat up and stretched himself, rubbing
his eyes. Then he cleared his throat and in a loud voice
began to declaim the ancient Lay of Bjarki that he used
often to recite in old times in the king's hall. It was like a
trumpet call in the clear morning air.

"Day is dawning,
   the cock claps its wings,
   time it is for thralls
   their tasks to tackle.
   Awake, now, awake!
   of friends the firmest
   and all the foremost
   of Adil's companions!

"Har, the hard-handed,
   and Rolf, the sharp-shooter;
   men of good birth
   that flee not in battle;
   not for wine I wake you,
   nor women's whisperings,
   but for the stern
   sport of shield-maidens."

As Thormod declaimed, so the men about the king's standard began to stir and many sat up, until at last it seemed as though the whole army was listening, for as he ended, a great shout of applause went up, and the king thanked him gravely for the poem and gave him a golden arm ring.

"This was a fair beginning to a fateful day," he said, "and it may be that there will be matter for more verses before the sun goes down."

After this, men broke their fast lightly with such food as they had brought with them and then stood to in ranks under their troop standards, waiting, while the sun rose behind them and flooded the valley below.

Helgi felt strangely empty, although he had forced

himself to swallow a crust of bread washed down with sour beer. He shifted restlessly in his place in the third rank of the guard, adjusting the straps of his shield and rubbing the sweat from his right hand so that he could get a better grip on the hilt of the sword that King Olaf had given him.

Young Harald, who was on his left, had bound the hilt of his sword to his wrist, in case he should lose the heavy weapon in the fighting. Most of the men about them also carried war axes or long-hafted spears, while out in front were bowmen and those armed with light throwing-spears, ready to greet the enemy with a deadly hail as soon as they came within range.

The king stood with the second rank beside his great war banner that was held up by Thord Folason on a gilded staff. The white standard with its embroidered gold cross stirred gently in the morning breeze. The king himself was clad in a short hauberk of ring mail and a gilt helm and he carried a white shield marked with a golden cross. Belted about his waist he wore his sword Hneitir, and he held a long *kesja*, which was a war ax with a spear blade projecting from its top.

Just then the pickets returned. They reported that the enemy was massing in the woods below and an advance party of about thirty mounted men was coming up the track toward Sticklestead, clearly scouting to obtain information of the king's forces and their dispositions.

"I know their leader," said one of the pickets. "It was Ram of Vigg, beyond Nidaros."

As the man spoke, Helgi's eye was caught by a glitter of weapons at the edge of the woods.

"Ram?" said the king. Then he turned and called

Thorarin the Icelander to his side. "Thorarin, my old friend," he said, "how many horses have we brought up from the camp?"

"About a score, lord," replied Thorarin.

"Good," said the king. "Now, they tell me that it is the custom in Iceland for farmers to give their housecarls a sheep to kill in autumn after the hay harvest. Thorarin, I make you a gift of this Ram. Take as many men with you as there are horses, and make sure that not a man of this patrol escapes to give news of us to the chieftains."

"That I shall do willingly, king," replied Thorarin.

He rode off with his chosen companions, and was back in less than half an hour with blood on his spear.

"The Ram and his lambs will bleat no more," he announced shortly, "but I think that there will be meat enough for salting before our shadows grow much shorter."

Helgi stared at his uncle in surprise. There was a strange gleam in the gray-haired merchant's eye as he dismounted and returned to his place in the ranks. Thorarin gave the boy a wink and said, "The fire lives long in ancient ashes."

"Why didn't you let me come with you?" asked Helgi. "I'm tired of this waiting."

"Never fear," replied Thorarin, "you will not have to wait long. And listen, boy, you are to stay in your ranks and not take too many chances. The swords of the enemy are not more fearful to me than your mother's tongue, if anything should befall you."

Helgi heard Bjorn the Marshal ask the king whether a troop of men should be sent to occupy the farm, but the king replied that it was to be a refuge for the wounded of both sides, as he had declared to the farmer. "Let Dag Ringsson lead part of his troop into the wood to watch our flank," he said. "We must have patience. If our enemies are taking their time to attack us, we shall take the opportunity and rest ourselves." And he gave the order that all the men should sit down in their ranks on the grass, and he lay down himself and rested his head on Finn Arnason's knees. After a while he dozed, for he had slept but little during the night.

"See how the king sleeps," said Helgi, "with his enemies close at hand."

"So it is to have faith and a clear conscience," said Thorarin. "It would go hard with me to do the same."

"Why, do you doubt that we shall win?" exclaimed Helgi. "The king has said that God is on our side."

Thorarin shrugged his shoulders. "Who can tell, except God himself," he answered. "And I think that the king knows more than he will say. After all, was not God on the side of His Son at the hill of Calvary?"

Helgi shook his head, puzzled. "It may be that we shall die, many of us," he said, "but I am certain that the king will overcome his enemies. And Thormod the Scald, at least, will live to see his victory, for the king himself promised as much."

Just then Harald, who was sitting a little apart, gave a gasp and pointed forward down the slope.

"Look," he cried. "The wood! Look at the wood!"

Helgi looked at the dark line of the woods below, and suddenly it seemed as if the edge of them had erupted in a shifting, glittering dance of movement, like a chain of metal shaken across the valley. Then he heard the dull, distant boom of the war horns, and the sunlight glanced off burnished helm and weapon as rank upon rank of the chieftains' army emerged from the woods and spread out in a steel crescent over the green meadows below the farm.

Soon it seemed as if the whole valley was filled with armed men as the enemy ranks formed up behind their standards.

"We are many times outnumbered," Bjorn muttered, but Thormod the Scald said, "We are the stronger, for our cause is just."

"Look, they are beginning to advance," said Thorarin. "My friend Finn, I think the time has come to wake the king."

Already most of the king's army had been roused by the sight of the advancing horde in the valley, and men were drawing swords and setting shields to rights on every side, but still the king slept peacefully with his head on Finn's knees.

"There was a time," said Finn, "when no one would have dared to waken him for peril of his life, but all the same I shall do so now," and he shook the king gently by the shoulder.

The king sat up and said sharply, "Why did you wake me, Finn, instead of letting me enjoy my dream?"

"Look before you, lord, and see how near our enemies are," replied Finn.

"Not so near but that it would have been better for me to be asleep," said King Olaf. "It was a good dream."

"What did you dream, king, that you think you have missed so much by being woken?" asked Finn.

The king lowered his voice to reply and Helgi strained

his ears in vain to catch the words, but he saw Finn frown and shake his head.

"I wonder what the king dreamed," he said to his uncle.

Thorarin shrugged his shoulders. "The king's dreams are not to be taken lightly," he said, "but there is often more than one way of reading a dream."

"Then you did hear," said Helgi. "Was it good or bad, this one?"

"I have said that such things are hard to read," replied Thorarin evasively, "and men who go into battle should not think too much about signs and portents."

"No evil is so great that it is not greater in the imagining," said Thormod the Scald. "I heard the king's dream and it seems to me a fair one. He dreamed that he was climbing a high ladder that reached all the way to Heaven, and he said that he had climbed to the topmost rung when Finn awoke him. There is no evil in that dream, for I think that it means that the king will climb to victory over his enemies."

"It will not be long before we know the answer," said Thorarin. "Already one can distinguish their standards."

"Those are the men of Rogaland and the West on their left," called Bjorn the Marshal to the king.

"They will be eager to avenge the death of Erling," remarked Thorarin in a low voice. "I wish the king would make haste and send after Dag Ringsson, for our right is weakened too much."

"Unless I am mistaken, that is the standard of Calf coming to meet us in the center of their line," Helgi heard the king say. "Those will be the men of the Tronderlaw with him." Then he turned to Finn Arnason, who was close behind him, and said, "It is not too late for you and Thorberg to leave me, Finn. It is a bitter thing for a man to have to fight against his own brother."

"Calf is a traitor, and I will gladly slay him with my own hands," Finn replied angrily, but Helgi thought that it was hard for a man to have to choose between his kinsfolk and his king.

There had been some delay in the advance of the enemy, for their right flank had lagged behind the center and left, and the line was halted to allow them to catch up.

"That is the standard of Thorir Hound," said Bjorn. "Those will be the Halogalanders and the men from the North on their right, and it seems as if they have come late."

"They will not be tardy in pressing their attack, from what I know of them," said Finn. "And see, now their line is moving forward once more."

Now the war horns of the enemy boomed loudly and a sound like a growl of thunder could be heard as their line swept onward, engulfing the farm of Sticklestead as a wave washes round a rock on the shore, and at last the sound broke on the ears of the king's men as the roar of a battle cry:

"Forward, forward, yeomen!"

"Stand fast, king's men, till I give the word," shouted the king, and they stood their ground firmly, watching the enemy come.

Already arrows were beginning to fall, though most fell short and stuck in the grass before them. Then a few dropped among the ranks with a soft hiss and a thud as they hit the ground or stuck quivering in a wooden shield. After a while the light shower grew to a hail, and men began to fall. Then spears, too, were flying through the air, and for the first time Helgi understood the scalds' *kenning* or descriptive phrase for battle as "storm of weapons," as he ducked behind his round shield. He tried to swallow, to overcome the dreadful impulse to yawn, but his mouth was too dry.

All this time the king's bowmen had stood with their arrows notched to the string, waiting; but now at a sign from Bjorn the bowstrings twanged together and a rush of arrows rose into the sky, to be followed by another and yet another, and a cheer went up as gaps appeared in the advancing line. But as fast as men fell in the ranks of the yeomen, others stepped forward to take their place, for their line was as deep as that of the king's army was thin.

The faces of the enemy could now be clearly seen, grim and purposeful, between the rims of their painted shields and the metal and leather of helmet and nose-piece. Helgi could see their standard, a dark red flag with some emblem marked upon it in black. Was it a bird?

Just then a spear struck Helgi's shield a sharp blow and glanced off to bury its point in the ground beside him. At once he put his sword under his shield arm and pulled the spear out, to hurl it back at the enemy. He aimed at the black-bearded face of a man in front of the standard, but the spear fell several paces short.

Then the king raised his long ax in signal and a war horn brayed loudly close beside, and then the cry went up as the whole line of the king's army began to move forward to meet the attack, spears and swords leveled and axes raised:

"Forward, Christ's men, Cross men, king's men!"

At once Helgi's yawning fearfulness and the empty feeling in his stomach disappeared. Instead he felt a surge of elation, as though he were lifted and carried forward on a mighty wave.

He saw the rank of their own bowmen fall back on either side, and then the men in front of him were closing with the enemy.

The air was filled with a confusion of sounds: the thunderous crash of shield against shield and the clash of meeting weapons; shouts of triumph and screams of pain; the deep, repeated call of the war horns; and the gasps and sobs of men locked together in a savage struggle for life.

Helgi saw a man before him with ax raised above his head, and he leaped to one side as the blade flashed in the sun. Then he gripped the hilt of his sword firmly and struck out with all his strength, remembering as he did so the often-repeated words of the master-at-arms at Nidaros: "Use the edge, boy, use the edge! It's not a stick, to be hitting the rump of a cow with!"

He felt the blade bite into something soft and yet resistant, and the man dropped his ax with a cry. Helgi did not wait to see if he was badly wounded, for another was coming at him on the right, a short, bearded fellow in ring mail whose spear was aimed at his chest. He twisted round to stop the point with his shield, but was just too late to catch it squarely, and the iron spearhead slid off and grazed his thigh. Almost without thinking, he brought his right arm across in a slashing backhand blow and caught the man's arm just below the shoulder, where the ring mail ended, and his wrist was jarred by the sword hilt as the blade grated against bone. The bearded man gave a shriek and dropped his spear, clasping his shoulder, and then Helgi struck at his ankle and he staggered and fell.

Helgi ran forward, drunk with elation. He was fighting his first battle and he was not afraid. What was more, he had met and overcome two of the king's enemies, and he felt now that nothing could stop him.

"Forward, king's men!" he shouted, and he waved his reddened blade in the air and struck his shield with it. "Forward, for Christ and King Olaf!"

"Come back, you crazy young fool," a voice called after him, and he turned to see his uncle Thorarin a few paces behind, engaged with a tall Norwegian in a leather coat.

"Come on, Uncle," he cried, "strike him down! We'll drive the traitors into the Trondheimsfjord."

"Keep to the line," shouted Thorarin. "The king is waiting for Dag Ringsson. Our right is falling behind. Stay with the—"

His words were cut short as the tall Norwegian lunged forward and caught him a ringing blow on the side of the head with his ax. He stood for a moment, as though puzzled; then his legs doubled under him and he fell, and his opponent raised the ax again for a final stroke.

Helgi shouted and threw his sword which, by a lucky chance, hit the leather-coated man on the elbow. He turned at once on the boy who now stood before him unarmed, but just as he was about to strike, his whole body seemed to jerk forward as if pulled by a string and he fell on his face across Thorarin with the feathered shaft of an arrow between his shoulders.

Helgi recovered his sword hastily and then tugged at his uncle's arm, but the hand was limp and lifeless.

"Uncle," he cried. "Uncle Thorarin!"

But there was no response, and just then a voice called out, "Guard yourself, Helgi," and the next moment he felt a smashing blow on the back of his head and he seemed to be falling headlong into a dark pit.

"He'll do well enough," he heard a voice saying. "These Icelanders have heads like rock," and then another replied, "It's the iron cap that saved his life, without a doubt."

His head was aching horribly, as though a hammer was striking inside it, but he opened his eyes and saw that he was among friends and the king was nearby. Thormod the Scald and Harald were sitting on the ground beside him.

"What has happened?" he asked, sitting up. "Is the battle over?"

"Not yet, by any means," replied Thormod. "The men of Trondheim have withdrawn to lick their wounds, that's all. On the left and in the center we have done well, but on the right things have gone against us. The king is trying to restore our line before attacking once again."

"Where is my uncle Thorarin?" asked Helgi.

"Oh, he'll be all right," said Harald. "Like yourself, he took a knock on the head that robbed him of his wits for the while, but not for long, you may be sure. It's a splendid battle, isn't it Helgi? I've killed more than I can count."

"Young cockerel," said Thormod. "Leave your crowing

till after the fighting is done. Deeds speak louder than words. And now I think the time has come for more deeds," he added as the war horns began to sound.

"Shield wall, king's men, shield wall," shouted the deep voice of Bjorn the Marshal, and the men in front of them began to form up in a line with overlapping shields on either side of the king's standard.

"I have made a verse, Helgi," said Harald. "Would you like to hear it?"

"Another time," answered Helgi, pressing his aching head with his hands.

"No, I'll tell you now. My brother thought I was too young to fight, you see," said Harald. "He wanted me to stay behind with the supplies and the horses. Now I have shown him that I am a man. This is my verse:

"I am bold to hold
my place in the battle line;
widows will weep;
I redden the shield with rage on the battlefield.
I, the young, war-glad scald
will not turn heel in fear for spears
when blows fly free;
men are matched fiercely in murderous meeting, I see."

"I dare say it's not a very good verse," he added, "but one doesn't have time to do much polishing. Thormod the Scald says that it shows promise. But I must leave you now. They are making ready to launch another attack."

"I'm coming with you," said Helgi. "Give me my iron cap."

He eased the helmet on gently over his throbbing head, but the pressure was too painful, so he took it off again.

"Better an ax in the brain than that," he said, and he left it on the grass, but took up his sword that was lying near and hurried to join the crowd of men forming up behind the shield wall.

The king was less than two paces away, next to the big banner held by Thord Folason. He now raised his ax and cried, "Forward!" and the war horns sounded and the line shields began to move.

"Forward, Christ's men, Cross men, king's men!" the cry went up along the line and was echoed back from the wooded slopes above the valley.

They could see the enemy line wavering in front of them.

"This will do it," shouted Thormod the Scald. "See, they are already shaken. One good push and the day is ours."

There was a sudden outburst of cheering away on the left. Finn Arnason exclaimed, "By the sword of St. Michael, if the heavenly powers are not on our side! They are fighting among themselves over there." And it was true, for some of the men of Halogaland, come late and breathless into the battle, had heard the war cry of the king's army and had taken it up themselves, and were at once attacked by the men of their own side in error.

"God has confounded our enemies and given us the victory," shouted the king, but his voice was lost in the crash of shields as the guard met the enemy center head on, and the next moments were a wild confusion of savage hand-to-hand fighting.

Helgi saw the king press forward in the melee, closely

followed by the standard-bearer, and he kept behind them, guarding his bare head with his shield as he fought through the broken ranks of the men of Trondheim. The king himself was fighting magnificently, his long-handled ax clearing the way before him with dreadful, sweeping blows. It seemed as if not one of his enemies dared stand before him or face the fearful anger in his eyes, for Helgi saw one man after another turn away from him. But at last one man, taller and more richly clad than the rest, stood squarely in front of him and did not falter, and under the nosepiece of the burnished helmet Helgi recognized the noble features of Calf Arnason.

The king spoke. "Well, Calf, we meet again," he said. "When we parted last, we were friends. It is ill done of you to join with my enemies, especially since your brothers are here with me."

"Many things go otherwise than we would wish, king," replied Calf, and he stepped back to guard himself with his long sword. "When we parted company, I had to make peace with those who were left behind. A man must stand firm in the place where he finds himself. Nevertheless, if I had my way there would be a truce between us now."

A voice called out, "When Calf speaks fair, then all may know that he means mischief," and Helgi turned to see that it was Calf's brother Finn who spoke.

"If you want peace, Calf," said the king, "then this is not the way to behave."

Then a dark, bearded man who had come up beside Calf called out, "You shall have the kind of peace that you have given others, king."

"Thorgeir of Kvistead," replied the king, "you should not be too eager to meet me. I raised you up from the dirt and made you a man of importance. But I tell you that victory will not be yours this day."

Helgi saw the king raise his ax and move forward, and then his attention was engaged elsewhere as the eddy of battle swirled round him. He saw young Harald exchanging blows with a man almost twice his height, and ran to his aid, but not before a swipe of the boy's sword had brought the man to the ground with severed leg tendon.

"Well done, Harald," he exclaimed.

"I think I have never enjoyed a day better, Helgi," Harald panted. His face was flushed and his eyes shining. "Already the peasants are turning tail," he said. "Look!"

It was true that things had gone well for the king on the left and in the center. Heartened by the confusion among the Halogalanders, the king's Swedish allies had pushed forward to the left of the farm, while many of the yeomen and small freeholders among the men of Trondheim had begun to lose heart because of the fierceness of the guards' attack, and already some were slipping away from the field of battle. But the hard core of housecarls and retainers from the chieftains' households stood firm; and away on the right of the king's army things were not going so well, for since part of Dag Ringsson's force of Norwegian exiles had been drawn off to cover the ridge against enemy infiltration, the weakened remainder were being swept back by the superior numbers of the men of Rogaland, Sogn and the Firths. These hardy, seagoing warriors from the west of Norway were fierce fighters, and many of them had looked to Erling

Skjalgsson as chief and were eager to avenge his death.

The king had held up his attack as long as he had dared, waiting for Dag to return. Messengers had been sent, but now the ridge was cut off by the advance of the westerners, and the attack had been launched for fear of losing the advantage of the moment.

Thus the king's center had driven a deep wedge into the enemy line at the risk of being outflanked. So far they had been able to hold their position, but many of the guard had fallen in the spearhead of the attack owing to the savage resistance of the housecarls, and now a new danger was threatening from the left. Thorir Hound had managed to regroup his Halogalanders in a firm line and, with fresh reinforcements, he was himself leading a bitter attack on the extended left flank of the king's advance. The king, fighting in the vanguard of the attack, saw at a glance that if the pressure slackened for an instant he and those with him might be cut off and surrounded by the weight of enemy numbers. Their only chance was to force a quick decision with the chieftains —triumph, or be destroyed.

The sun was now high overhead and Helgi was sweating freely under his bearskin. Also his head was throbbing painfully and the graze on his left thigh had begun to smart and swell and the knee was growing stiff. He was so weary that he scarcely had strength to lift his sword and would have given his dearest possession to have been able to lie down and rest on the spot. But there was no respite. Blows were falling like hail, and his shield arm was aching abominably with the effort of warding them off. He saw the standard out of the corner of his eye—torn and cut in several places, but still held proudly aloft by Thord Folason—and he hobbled toward it. His uncle Thorarin was there and gave him a smile when he saw him. There was a small band of the guard there, fighting about the king: Finn Arnason, Thormod, Bjorn the Marshal and others. Harald was with them, but he was sitting in the grass with blood running from a gash on his leg. The king had lost his ax and was fighting now with his sword, and it flashed in the sun as he laid about him.

Helgi saw the dark, bearded man, whom the king had named Thorgeir of Kvistead, fall to a slashing blow across the face that sheared right through the nosepiece of his helmet, and the king called out, "What did I say, Thorgeir? I told you that victory would not be yours this day!"

Then Thord Folason was struck in the chest by an arrow, and he gave a great cry and, lifting the staff which held the king's standard, he drove it with all his strength into the ground, so that it stood upright, but he fell dead beneath it.

At this moment there was a cheer behind them and someone called out that Dag Ringsson was come and was driving the westerners before him like sheep to market.

"He has left it late," cried the king and then, as he turned to face a dark-looking man with a cloak of reindeer skin about his shoulders, he said, "Thorir Hound, this meeting has been too long delayed," and he raised his sword and cut at Thorir; but the blow bounded off the reindeer skin, raising a cloud of dust, and Thorir was not hurt. Then Thorir Hound drove at the king with a long spear that he carried, and King Olaf warded off the point with his shield, and the two exchanged several fierce cuts and thrusts, and although Thorir was wounded on the hand, each time the king struck at his body the blow was turned.

"Devilish sorcerer," muttered the king, "your Finnish spells will not save you from the wrath of God!" Then he called out aloud to Bjorn the Marshal, saying, "Come hither with your ax, Bjorn, and beat the hound that steel cannot bite."

Bjorn came up and lifted his great ax, turning it in his hands so that the hammerhead at the back of the blade pointed downward, and he brought it down with all his strength on the shoulder of Thorir Hound, so that he reeled at the blow. At the same instant Calf Arnason came to the aid of Thorir with another man, and the king turned quickly and dealt Calf's companion a death wound, but Thorir Hound had a moment in which to recover, and he jabbed his spear at Bjorn's belly, crying as he did so, "This is how we bait bears in the north!"— for the name *Bjorn* means "bear" in the Norse tongue.

Bjorn the Marshal sank to the ground, mortally wounded. Then a man named Thorstein Shipwright attacked the king. He was a great merchant and a skilled craftsman who had a grudge against King Olaf because he had once taken a ship from him, newly built and ready for sea, on account of his deeds of piracy. Thorstein now struck at the king with an ax and wounded him on the left leg above the knee. Finn Arnason at once sprang forward and felled Thorstein, killing him outright, but King Olaf leaned against a large stone that stood in that place and, throwing down his sword, called upon God to help him.

At that moment a terrible thing happened, so that Helgi, who stood near the king, felt his bones turn to water.

The sun, which up to now had blazed out of a clear blue sky with a heat that made the sweat run down his body in the effort of battle, was suddenly darkened, and the air grew chill. He glanced up quickly and all but dropped his sword when he saw a rim of blackness eating into the bright orb. Cries of amazement and terror rang out as men raised their faces to the eclipse and held up their arms to shield their eyes from the darting brightness of the flames that seemed to leap from the sun's edge. Then the valley was plunged in darkness and birds flew up from the woods about them and circled overhead with plaintive cries of alarm.

But before the last pale twilight had drained away, Thorir Hound rushed forward and thrust his spear into the king below his coat of ring mail—the spear, men said, that had been the death of his kinsman Asbjorn Seals-bane—and at the same time Calf Arnason gave his former master and king a blow on the left side of the neck, and King Olaf slid to the ground and lay still.

To the End of Time

Helgi opened his eyes to find himself in half darkness. His body was aching all over, and the air around him was filled with groans and heavy breathing. He seemed to be in some kind of a building. There was straw underneath him and the dim outline of rafters above his head.

He sat up painfully and looked about him. In the faint

glow of a brazier on the earthen floor of the barn—for
such it seemed to be—he could see men lying on all sides
in attitudes of agony and exhaustion. A group stood talking together in low voices by the fire, and women were
hurrying back and forth, with water in bowls, and cloths
and other articles of the leech's trade.

Finding himself with no serious wound, though
bruised and stiff in every limb, Helgi crawled on hands
and knees toward the open space by the fire, ignoring the
groans of protest from those whom he touched in passing,
for he was anxious to hear what the men there were saying. By now he realized that the wounded in the barn
were from both armies, though more seemed to be king's
men; but he was still uncertain about the final outcome
of the battle—if, indeed, it was yet over.

When he came within earshot of the men round the
brazier he heard one of them saying that Dag Ringsson's
attack had carried all before it until the sudden darkness
of the eclipse had brought it to an end in confusion and
uncertainty.

"When the sun returned," said the man, "it was to show
Dag and his troop in full flight before the westerners."

"Ay," said another, "and if what I heard is true, they
will not stop running until they reach the top of Veradale
and the Swedish border."

"Thorir Hound has gone out after them with a force
of his own men," said the first man. "He means to make
sure that not one of the Norwegian exiles returns to
trouble the land again."

"Yet he and Calf Arnason have ordered that there is
to be no looting," remarked a third man.

"Have you heard how Calf looked for his brothers Finn

and Thorberg among the king's party?" asked another. "All but a handful of those about the king's standard had fallen, dead or wounded, or were so weary that they could scarcely hold their weapons. Finn and Thorberg were there, still alive, and Finn had the strength left to throw his knife at his brother Calf, calling him a traitor and a truce-breaker. Calf had them both carried off to his ship down in the fjord."

"Most of the men of Trondheim left the field with him," grumbled a man who spoke with the accent of the West Fjords, "eager to get back to their farms and leave the dirty work to others."

"What do you expect?" asked the man who had spoken about Calf. "The battle had all but come to a standstill by that time, and when news got round that the king had fallen, many on both sides were ready to lay down their arms."

Helgi noticed that when he spoke of the king, even this man of the chieftains' army lowered his voice respectfully.

"I heard a strange tale about Thorir Hound," said a dark-looking warrior who had stood apart from the rest up to this time. "It seems that he came, after the battle, to where the king lay, to make sure that he was dead, and when he wiped the blood from the king's face, his cheeks were as fresh and ruddy as if he were still alive."

"Well, what of that?" said the westerner. "Men will sometimes look so when they are dead."

"Thorir had been wounded on the hand," said the other, ignoring the interruption. "He covered the king's face with a cloth, and it seems that some of the blood came onto his hand, and all at once his wound dried up, leaving no more than a faint scar."

"You northerners are ever ready to believe tales of marvels," said the man from the west scornfully, "just as there are some who say that Thorir is himself a sorcerer and shields himself from earthly weapons by the magic of the Finns."

"And so it is true," exclaimed the dark man angrily. "He is a bold man who will tell me that I lie—"

Just then the doorway darkened and the figure of a man appeared in it, and those by the fire broke off their conversation.

Helgi saw that the newcomer was Thormod the Scald. *So the king had been mistaken after all, when he said that he and Thormod would not be parted,* he thought.

One of the leechwomen attending the wounded now came up to Thormod as he stood by the door and said that if he was not himself in need of leechcraft he should go out and fetch some firewood from the stack outside. Thormod went out and came back a minute later with an armful of wood which he threw down on the floor. Then the leechwoman looked at him more closely.

"How pale you are," she said. "Is there anything the matter with you?"

Thormod answered her question with a verse:

> "The fair bearer of hawks
> remarks that the poet is pale.
> Few grow handsome of wounds.
> I met the arrow-flight, maiden.
> The well-aimed shaft, with craft

fiercely shot, has pierced me.
The deadly iron bites deep;
close to my heart its dart."

"Let me see your wound," said the woman, and Thormod sat down and pulled off his clothes. Helgi could see the broken shaft of an arrow protruding from his side, but there was little bleeding.

"Hallo, Thormod," he said. "You are hurt."

"Hallo, boy," said Thormod. "It is nothing to be making a fuss about, I reckon."

"The king is dead," said Helgi.

"Yes," replied Thormod in a colorless voice. "The king is dead."

"Now you stop talking and eat some of this," said the leechwoman, "and we'll see how deep that arrow has gone." She handed Thormod a bowl containing a mess of garlic and other herbs, meaning to tell by the scent of the herbs after he had eaten whether or not the lung was pierced.

Thormod looked at the bowl and said, "Take it away. My sickness is not a craving for vegetable soup. Bring your pincers to me," he added, "and I shall pull out the arrowhead."

The woman did as he had bidden her, and he took a gold ring from his arm and handed it to her.

"This is a worth-while gift," he said. "King Olaf gave it to me himself this morning."

Then, bidding Helgi support him, he gripped the broken shaft of the arrow firmly with the pincers and drew out the arrowhead, and the blood welled from the wound.

"See," he said, examining the barbs of the arrow, "see, there is fat about my heart. King Olaf has fed us well."

Then he fell back dead.

Helgi wept unashamedly. "He was my fellow country-man and my friend," he told the leechwoman. "The king said that they would not be parted. . . ."

The next morning Helgi left the barn, with little idea where he should go, but thinking maybe that he could find the sword that King Olaf gave him, which was lost on the field of battle.

As he limped painfully up the track from the farm, he saw that already the dead had been taken away, though the grass was still trampled and bloodstained and there were broken weapons and shields lying scattered every-where. There was a newly dug mound beside the track, and a man with a handcart was out searching the mead-ows for arms and other objects of value; otherwise the valley seemed to be deserted, and lay peaceful between the hills in the clear morning sunshine.

Then he heard a voice behind him, and there was his uncle, his gray hair blowing in the light breeze.

"How glad I am to see you," said Thorarin, hurrying up to him and embracing him warmly. "When I could not find you among the wounded I was sure that you were dead."

"Thormod is dead," said Helgi.

"I know," said his uncle with a sigh. "And so are many other good men this day. Things have not gone well with us."

"What about Harald?" asked Helgi. "I saw him wounded."

"I have heard that he is safe," replied Thorarin. "He

fled on horseback with Dag Ringsson and those of his men who escaped up the valley. By this time they are probably in Sweden."

"What will happen to us?" Helgi asked the question dully, as though it were a matter of little concern to him.

"Calf Arnason has given safe conduct to all foreigners who were with the king to leave the country," replied Thorarin. "You shall come with me to Nidaros and we shall buy a passage home to Iceland. I have money enough for the two of us there. I sold my ship in Sweden for the king's cause, but I think that my sailing days are over."

They had come now to the stone on the battlefield by which the king had fallen, and Helgi was on his knees in the grass, rummaging about among the litter of weapons.

"My sword," he explained, turning his face away so that Thorarin should not see the tears that had suddenly filled his eyes. "I want to keep it, because . . . *he* gave it to me."

At last he found it, rusted with blood and dew, and wrapped it carefully round with fragments of a tattered cloak that lay nearby.

"What have they done with him?" he asked.

Thorarin shook his head and said, "Maybe we can find out at the farm. Come, let us leave this place and be on our way." And he took Helgi gently by the arm and led him down the hill again.

They met Thorgils, the farmer, outside his cowshed. He looked frightened and suspicious at their approach, but then he recognized Thorarin for one of the friends of King Olaf and his brow lightened.

"It's you," he said. "I thought they had come back. They came last night looking for him, but they'll get nothing out of me, though it cost me the farm and my life as well."

"You are an honest man, Thorgils," said Thorarin. "Had I the means I would reward you better for it. But take this. . . ." and he drew a gold ring from his finger and handed it to the farmer.

Thorgils looked at the ring in the palm of his hand and said, "I will put it together with the silver that he gave me for Masses."

"I think that King Olaf has little need of Masses where he is now," said Helgi quietly, "but take this, too, Master Thorgils, both for him and for his friends who went with him. It is all that I have." And he gave the farmer his purse with the little silver that he had kept against an emergency.

"May we see him?" asked Thorarin, but the farmer shook his head.

"My son Grim and I have hidden him where they will not find him," he answered. "Later we shall convey him to a safer place, so that he can have decent Christian burial."

"Who is this, that comes running after us over the meadow?" asked Helgi. "It seems that he has news of importance to tell us."

"It is Grim," replied Thorgils. They turned and watched the young man who was coming toward them, waving his arms and calling on them to stop. "What in heaven's name can ail him?"

When Grim came up with them he gasped that he must speak with his father alone.

"I have no secret from these friends of King Olaf," said Thorgils, "if it is aught to do with him."

Grim glanced about him nervously and said, "It is about the blind beggar that I would speak, Father, the one that sought food and shelter from us last night."

"Well, what of him?" said his father impatiently. "There are always many such that come in the wake of armies, like ravens after the plow, for what they can beg or pick up."

"I told him that he could sleep in one of the outbuildings," said Grim, "and it seems that he went to the very shed to which we carried *him* under cover of darkness."

"Well, there was no harm in that," said Thorgils. "After we had washed and laid out the body we took it from that place."

"Yes, Father, but now he has come to me with a strange story, and all the people of the farm know about it," replied Grim. "He says that when he lay down to sleep in the shed, his hat fell off his head and into a pool of water on the floor—or such he thought it was—so that when he picked up the hat his fingers were wet. And then he chanced to rub his eyes with his fingers, and at once they began to smart. After that he went out of the shed, thinking to find a drier place, and suddenly it seemed to him that he could see the buildings about him, although it was dark. At first he thought that maybe this was some kind of dream or illusion of the night; then later he saw the stars and knew that he was no longer blind, and there was blood on his hands."

"This is a strange thing," said Thorarin after a long silence. "Maybe the man was not blind after all."

"He is well known in the district and has been blind many years," said Thorgils.

"And now he sees clearly, like any other man," said Grim.

Again there was a silence, and the three looked at one another almost with fear in their eyes.

"Uncle," said Helgi at last, "once you told me of a dream that the king dreamed many years past, south in the land of Spain, in which one told him to return to his own land and claim his birthright."

"That is so," said Thorarin with a sigh. "But the one in his dream promised that he would be king of Norway to the end of time, and now his reign has ended, and there seems to be little hope even that his own kin will wear the crown after him. Why do you speak of that now?"

Helgi had turned away and was gazing up the valley, past the farm of Sticklestead, shielding his eyes with his arm against the blaze of the sun.

"How beautiful it is, this land of Norway," he said. "Uncle, if I were a Norwegian do you know what I would say?"

"How should I know that, boy?" said his uncle, putting a hand on his shoulder. "What would you say then, Helgi?"

"I would say that the reign of King Olaf Haraldsson was not ended. It is only just beginning."

A Note on History and Story

After King Olaf's death people began to tell many stories of cures and miracles, like the healing of the blind man at Sticklestead. Soon Bishop Grimkel heard about them—he had been allowed to keep his see in Upland—and he came north to Trondheim to inquire into them, and also to find out what had happened to the king's body after the battle.

It seems that Thorgils Halmuson and his son Grim had buried it in a sandbank in the river near Nidaros, and the bishop had it exhumed with the permission of King Svein Knutsson, who was now ruling over Norway in the name of his father, Knut of Denmark. The body looked fresh and rosy, as if the king had just fallen asleep. It was carried to the church of St. Clement in Nidaros and placed in a shrine above the high altar, and soon it became an object of pilgrimage. Later a cathedral was built in Olaf's honor, and pilgrims flocked there from every land in the north. The king who had been driven out of his country by his own people was now hailed as a saint and a martyr both in Norway and beyond. Even in England churches were dedicated in his name within a few years of his death.

Among the first to acknowledge St. Olaf's sanctity were some of those Norwegian chieftains who had opposed him so bitterly during his lifetime. Perhaps they soon found that the change of masters had not left them with the greater freedom which they had hoped for and that the outcome of their self-willed rebellion and disunity had only been to expose their country to the tyranny and misrule of foreigners—the Danes. The common people certainly found themselves worse off and looked back with regret to the days of King Olaf's stern but equal justice that had so often stood between them and the arbitrary power and violence of the chiefs. In this way the name and cult of St. Olaf became a sort of rallying point of Norwegians, both rich and poor, against the foreigner, and created for the first time in history something like a sense of Norwegian nationhood. About five years after Sticklestead, Olaf's son, Magnus, was called out of his exile in Russia with the common consent of all Norwegians to resume the crown of his father.

But King Olaf's greatest achievement was to complete the work of converting Norway to the Christian Faith, begun by his predecessor Olaf Tryggvason. During his reign Norway ceased to be a missionary land and became one of the kingdoms of medieval Christendom. Controversial though his life was his valiant labors on behalf of the Church in Norway which wiped out paganism there are his true mark in history.

The Scandinavian lands were the last outpost of heathenism in western Europe—it was some years before the Swedes accepted the Faith—but in later ages all these countries: Norway, Sweden, Denmark, Iceland, and Finland too, adopted as part of their national emblems the cross that St. Olaf had chosen as his sign at Sticklestead.

Of the characters in this story, only Helgi the Icelander is imaginary. All the others appear in the *Life of St. Olaf* written many years later by another Icelander, Snorri Sturluson. Snorri based his book partly on the verses of poets such as Sigvat, which had been remembered and passed on.

It is said that Thorir Hound was filled with remorse at his part in the killing of the king, and went on a pilgrimage to Jerusalem soon after.

Calf Arnason became the friend and protector of the king's son, Magnus, staying with him in exile and returning with him to Norway when he was called to be king in 1035.

Sigvat the Scald was in Rome when he heard about King Olaf's death and was overwhelmed with grief that he had not been with his master at the time. Later he returned to Norway to serve King Magnus.

Harald, the half-brother of King Olaf, lived to rule Norway after Magnus and gained the nickname *Hardrada,* or the tyrant, because of his stern ways. He was a better warrior than king and belonged to the old viking tradition. He died in a raid on England; being defeated by his namesake, the English king Harold Godwinsson, at Stamford Bridge in the year 1066, a few days before the landing of William of Normandy at Hastings.

The King's Men

Iceland

Faeroe Is.

Shetland Is.

Orkney Is

Scotland

W N E S